The Mortal One

Shannon Bell

The Mortal One
Copyright © 2013 by Shannon Bell
All rights reserved.

This is a work of fiction. All of the characters, organizations, and events portrayed in this novel are either products of the author's imagination or are used fictitiously. Any resemblance to actual events, locales, or persons, living or dead, is entirely coincidental.

Book design by Sprinkles on Top

ISBN: 978-0-9913341-0-0

DEDICATION

Thank you to every paranormal romance writer that came before me, inspiring me with tales of vampires and the other things that go bump in the night.

This book is dedicated to my family, who always supported me and asked me for the first autographed copy, even before I wrote the first word.

THE MORTAL ONE

ACKNOWLEDGMENTS

This book would have never been possible if it weren't for the constant nagging of my friends inside the FWA and my mom begging me for new chapters (and cursing me when I would keep her waiting too long). I'm also grateful to my critique group in Kissimmee– the book would not be what it is today without everyone's comments and suggestions.

I also thank everyone who has ever responded to questions about Romania, Paris, and Florence on the many internet boards.

Chapter 1

DESPITE MY CHILDHOOD fascination with vampires, I needed to get the hell out of Transylvania. As if the shitty Vampire Symposium wasn't confirmation enough, the man in front of me who had a silver blade jutting out of a goat's throat pretty much summed up everything.

We were off the beaten path, literally. The dark sky streaked with purple clouds matched my mood. I silently begged for the night to come quickly to a close so the train could collect me the next morning. I'd take whatever the train station had – the earlier the better.

"Do you want to drink?" The tall man with deep set eyes held a goblet under the dying goat's neck that collected thick, red blood.

I shuddered in horror. "That is so *not* what I had in mind when you invited me out here, Alin."

"Stop being such a girl, Dylan. You wanted to know how vampires lived, so here it is."

Let me back up for a moment. I met Alin at the hotel bar the day the symposium ended. He appealed to all of the dark senses I had about vampires and told me that he was one. In foolish naivety, I fell for it. He offered to show me the other side of how he lived and now here I was, miles away from the gothic churches with their ornate steeples, the gas-burning street lamps of Brasov, and any civilization whatsoever. My life had been filled with idiotic choices over the years, but this one made it to the very top of the list.

My attention was split between Alin and the other guy with him. I didn't catch his name and I wasn't going to bother asking at this point. It wasn't like we were going to be best friends anytime in the near future.

"She thought you meant real vampires, Alin," the shorter, pock-faced man commented. "Look at her face."

I stood tall while pulling at my reddish brown pony tail and wishing like hell my legs would carry me as fast as I wanted to run. Instead, my knees locked in place and my eyes met his. "I'm not drinking that. It's been a long night. Can you just take me back to my hotel already?"

Alin let out a rich, hearty laugh, which told me that he didn't care about me and thought this whole stunt was very amusing. It shook me to my core and pissed me off each second he continued. "Just as soon as we're done here. There's no sense wasting good goat's blood because you're disappointed that real vampires don't exist."

"Is the blood really necessary?"

The two men looked at each other as if they considered stopping for a moment. Then they both responded with a simultaneous, "Yes."

Alin decided to elaborate. "The goat's blood symbolizes life. As vampires, we must take life in order to enjoy life. Just be thankful that it's a goat each month we sacrifice instead of a human."

My blood was rising an extra degree as it coursed through my flushed cheeks. My emotions were starting to betray me but refused to let some fake vampire cult make me cry. I am twenty-eight years old, damn it – I am *not* going to cry.

"Dylan, you had to know that I wasn't the kind of vampire you thought."

My cheeks flushed. *Please don't go there.*

"The kissing…," he trailed off.

Pock Face chose now to chime in. "Alin, you didn't tell me that you kissed her."

"Shut up," we both demanded in unison.

My avid reading of vampire literature over the years taught me three truths that always remained the same. One, vampires only came out at night. Two, they had fangs. Three, they were cold to the touch.

I should have known better with Alin because he only met one of the three truths: I only saw him at night. The kisses we stole in the booth in the back of the hotel bar told me that he was very warm to the touch. I used enough tongue to know he didn't have any fangs, too, but I had rationalized. Maybe he had fed recently enough to give him the warmth. He also could have had retractable fangs for all I knew.

My life seemed to be crumbling around me back in Florida. Something had to change. Nothing was keeping me in the States and I could finally pursue other interests. The symposium was *supposed* to be the catapult that sent my life into some sort of meaningful direction.

"You and I aren't that different, you know," Alin spoke.

My gaze narrowed on him. "What do you mean?"

"We both seek the truth. I'm giving you the vampires you wanted. It took me a long time to realize they don't exist in the form you were hoping for. I was a member of the Transylvanian Society for years. Truth seekers are out there, but most of them give up at some point or another."

My lips thinned as I contemplated his words. I didn't want to give up yet I knew that most of what he said was right.

"Did you get anything out of the symposium that was actually helpful?"

"No," I admitted.

"There you go," he remarked, satisfied in his revelations.

Pock Face straddled the goat and held its thrashing body in place so Alin could get the remaining blood from its throat.

The men drank the thick, red fluid steadily for the next few minutes before they wiped their lips, laughed, and carried on. The goat collapsed in a heap with a final wheeze. Pock Face kicked it and Alin made a gesture towards me that let me know they were finally ready to take me back to my hotel.

I sat in silence and cursed at myself the whole way back while mentally devising my travel plans. My original itinerary had me scheduled here until Friday, but it was only Tuesday night and I already wanted to leave. There were trains that would get me out of here tomorrow morning if only I could manage to get on one of them.

***

"You were at the Vampire Symposium this past weekend, yes?" A female voice with a thick Eastern European accent caught me off guard as I unloaded my luggage onto the train.

I nodded and took a seat. "Yeah, though I wish I hadn't wasted my money."

She nodded and reached across the aisle with her arm extended. "I am Eva."

My hand met hers. "Dylan."

"I come every year and hope each time that it will get better. Is this your first year?"

"Yep, and my last. I've been a member of the Transylvanian Society for Dracula since high school. I've wanted to go to the conference each time I saw their notices, but school and life kept getting in the way and it's expensive to fly all the way out here."

She fumbled through her backpack and took out a journal, which she set down next to her. "I can imagine. It is hard enough for me to gather up the funds and I am only a country away. Where in the US are you from?" Her long fingers combed through the short blond spikes of her hair as she waited for my response.

"Florida," I said, leaning back and getting comfortable. It was a long ride and I was just glad to be out of Romania.

I had loved everything about it when I first arrived to Romania. The train ride from Bucharest to Brasov was astonishing. The green meadows with the alluring Carpathians in the background made me glad that I got away from my job as a restaurant manager for a little while. My best friend Jen was pissed that I was leaving her for three weeks but she'd get over it.

"You're a long way from home," Eva commented.

I nodded. "Yeah. This trip was much needed. My passport has never been stamped before so I figured it was time to change all that. I'm headed to Paris and then Florence for a little while longer before I go back home."

"Wonderful! I am just outside of Budapest and never seem to travel. My boyfriend gives me a hard time when I come here every year." She was fumbling with her journal again but I didn't bother to ask about it. "So did you see any vampires?" She asked, now clutching the leather binding.

My mouth gaped open for a moment as she so leisurely asked the question. "Excuse me?"

"What? I see them from time to time. Did you not meet Alin and his crew?"

I laughed and wanted to die all at the same time. At least I wasn't the only one who had ever been duped by them.

"Oh yeah. We became great friends," I said sarcastically. "Do you know them personally?"

She handed her journal to me where she had several newspaper clippings about the supposed vampire cult they had created in Brasov. "It is a popular cult they run. Every year at the symposium they get a few new recruits. You did not want to join?"

"Absolutely not. I've never wanted to leave a country so bad in all of my life."

Eva and I talked about the Vampire Symposium for a while, both wishing we hadn't wasted our money. We exchanged email addresses and promised to keep in touch. I switched trains for Paris, which was just fifteen hours away, once she got off in Budapest. Half asleep, my head leaned against the glass window and my breath formed clouds on the glass in front of me. My eyes had become heavy and the last thing I remembered seeing was the bright, yellow flowers scattering the meadows of Switzerland, a sure sign that spring was here.

Chapter 2

THE TRAIN EVENTUALLY stopped in Paris and I breathed a sigh of relief. France. Things would be better in France. There was no symposium or anything to bring me down. My time here was all about sightseeing and relaxing. Maybe now the inheritance I got from the death of my parents six months ago wouldn't be completely wasted. With luggage in tow, I found the terminal to be busier than expected.

A thirty-something year old woman was struggling to open a stroller for her screaming child. I tried to go around but her wide hips, the stroller, and the diaper bag left no room. I saw a bathroom and figured that it was a good excuse to let her do her thing without getting me too upset in the process. I shoved past a few more people with bags and stood in front of the sinks to splash cold water on my face. I needed to wake up. Staring into the mirror revealed a tired version of myself. My light skin was slightly red as my makeup had faded from the long train ride. My freckles were more visible without the foundation. Lines formed under my eyes, too, and my eyeliner was smeared.

I cranked out some paper towels and dampened them in the sink to wipe the smudges. My blue eyes were usually the first thing people complimented me on. Today, however, they looked faded from sheer exhaustion.

With a few elbows and a few *"pardonnez moi's,"* I was on my way out of the bathroom and attempting to get outside of the terminal. After finding a quiet corner, I pulled the map out of my back pocket to see where I needed to go.

My hotel wasn't that far away, but it wasn't really in walking distance. The phone showed that I could take a bus and then the metro, so that's what I did. God I loved technology sometimes. The bus took me to the metro station and from there I went to the *Republique* station.

My hotel was finally in sight. Although it was hidden within a much larger building, the purple doors made it stand out. Flags from over a dozen different countries hung from the top of the awnings and invited me in. I was hoping one of them was from an English speaking country in case my how-to CDs weren't as good as they claimed to be. The hotel wasn't much to look at, but it was close to everything.

I stepped through the heavy wooden double doors paneled with glass ovals and was thrilled to see the website didn't lie. A faint jazz piano quickened my step and the airiness of the lobby greeted me. It was paneled with dark mahogany and there was the scent of fresh-baked cookies in the air.

The man at the front desk stood stoic and watched me lug my bags across the lobby floor. I guess he had no intentions of helping me. I hoped I was putting on a good show for him.

After a few words in French and cheating with some English thrown in, he was able to find my reservation. "Dylan Monohan?" The male clerk, Jean, sounded out each syllable ever so slowly.

"Yes." My tone was probably a little angrier than it should have been but the fatigue was spilling over. I wanted nothing more to get into my room so I could land face first onto the bed.

"Is that your husband's name?"

I sighed. I was in no mood for this. I was tired of people assuming I was a guy all the time just by hearing my name. "Non." I couldn't translate the rest of what I wanted to say so I opted for a smile and asked, "Do you want to see my ID?"

He shook his head and pushed my room card at me. I reached for one of the cookies on the counter and headed towards the elevator with cookie in mouth and bags in both hands. The man at the desk obviously wasn't going to help, though he did seem amused. I didn't care. At this point, all I wanted was a clean room, a hot shower, and a bed.

There was no alarm clock in the room, which I was actually happy about. I took the next morning to sleep in, catching up on the deprivation of the past few days. Twenty-six hours on trains wasn't the way I wanted to spend part of my European vacation but at least it wasn't Romania. So much of my childhood and early adulthood was spent fantasizing about what Romania would be like – after all, it was the land of vampires. Until the symposium, it had lived up to it. All the talk there of creating Dracula Land, a vampire-themed amusement park blew those images to hell. Vampires had always held a curiosity for me. As for Alin, well, I had hoped that he was the real deal. I wanted him to be in such a huge way that I found it hard to explain, even to myself. But in the end, Alin had disappointed me worse than Romania had.

The room I was in was worth the money. It had some stunning features that I did not take the time to notice yesterday. The windows were covered with a pale gauzy material and gold and cream paisley curtains hung ornately at the sides. Peering out the window, I noticed there wasn't much of a view – unless you counted the stone gray commercial building across the street, which I didn't.

The main thing I wanted to do today was to see the Eiffel Tower. Cliché? Of course it was, but it wouldn't change anything. Before leaving the hotel, my body craved another shower like the one from last night. I savored every moment the state-of-the-art shower head beat rhythmically over my body. It was just what was needed. Paris, here I come.

I had to stand in line for two hours just to get to the top of the Tower. The view was worth it but the locals weren't very friendly in the gift shops. This meant that I still had to find somewhere to buy postcards. If I didn't, friends back home may never talk to me again.

After that it was on to the Panoramic Tour of Paris. I cheated a little by opting for the English language selection on the tour. I sat back in an air-conditioned bus instead of walking everywhere, relaxed, and watched the sights pass by. During the ride, there was so much to see including the *Arc de Triomphe* and a few other sights the city had to offer.

When the tour came to a stop at the Square des Innocents, I chose to hop off and take a walk for a while. *The Fountaine des Innocents* was a gorgeous fountain that had a lot of ornate decoration. I made a promise to Jen to take a photo of it for her and I have to admit that it was worth seeing in person.

From there, it was a short walk down the Boulevard de Sebastopol where I headed into a little patisserie for a few chocolate truffles. Indulgent, yes, but it *was* Paris, after all.

After leaving the patisserie, I wandered the streets and came face to face with the Church of St-Merri. With its stained glass windows of the nativity scene and the crowds of people worshipping the sacred ground, I stood numb. My efforts at avoiding a church for the past nine months came crumbling down.

In September of last year, my fiancé, Chris, had left me at the altar. Decked in a strapless white gown that had cost my parents a fortune, I stood before friends and family to marry my high school sweetheart. We'd been dating for twelve years. As I stared down the aisle through the open doors and waited for him to walk in, I could still hear the pianist playing the music over and over.

Only Chris never arrived. Jen, my maid of honor and Chris' sister, was worried that he had been involved in a car accident on the way to the church. After about an hour of frantic calls, his best man called from a local bar and told us that it wouldn't happen. I spent the next few days waiting for an explanation from Chris but one never came. I moved out of his apartment in silence. He never even gave his sister a reason for calling off the wedding.

Staring at the church reminded me of how much I hated Chris and would never get involved with someone to the point of marriage ever again. Why suffer heartbreak when I didn't have to?

I left St-Merri as I did the church in Florida – in tears. I couldn't step inside one yet. The emotions were still too raw. Chris was the only man I had ever loved. He had his flaws, yes, but he was all I ever had.

***

Hunger drove me out of my hotel room later in the evening. I found a little bistro with a menu written in French and English, which was a plus. I was hoping to get a better dinner than the stale croissant I had for lunch.

I knew a good meal would fuel me for my late evening walk, where I would finally enjoy peace. Everyone had either hit the city center for the night clubs or retreated to their hotels. I laid out a map of the city across my table and traced my finger along the different routes while making mental notes of the street names and necessary turns. I read the captions of the different buildings and thought about my trip.

Visiting the symposium was something I had wanted to do for years. It actually prompted the entire vacation. But the idea of vampires existing was what pushed it a little further. Before meeting Chris, I had fantasized about vampires and their real existence because there was too much literature and film out there about them for them *not* to exist. As Alin said, there are truth seekers who have dedicated their entire lives to finding the truth. While I wasn't about to give up my existence to find them, it was worth a few weeks to entertain my fantasies.

Vampires and their seductive powers, strength, and immortality captured my attention more than anything else did. Between the lectures by various "experts" in Romania and then Alin, though, I knew they didn't exist...not in the way I had always hoped, anyway. It stung, but I wasn't going to let it ruin my vacation.

The waiter delivered my Cassoulet, a chunky stew that made my stomach growl with the thick beef smell wafting from it. I grabbed my spoon and dug in.

In a way, a part of me wished Jen had gotten her way and came with me. Then again, this trip was about me and it was important to remember that. I remembered my promise to call her every few days and realized we hadn't spoken since before Alin entered the picture. Now it was Friday and I knew she'd be worried if I didn't call. I reached into my purse and grabbed my phone.

I got her voicemail and realized why when I glanced

at my watch. It was eight in the evening here, which meant that it was only two by her. She would be at work.

"Hey, you're probably working. Just wanted to let you know I'm in Paris early. I'll explain everything when I can catch up with you in the next few days. I promise to pay attention to the time change when I call again."

I waved my waiter over for a check. He dug in his apron for a few seconds before he produced it for me.

"*Bonne nuit*," he said as he set it on the table.

With my messenger bag slung across my shoulder, I tossed a few Euros on the table to take care of my bill and the waiter.

Some light traffic buzzed by and the sparkling lights of the Eiffel Tower flashed back and forth like a disco ball. It reminded me of the light shows at the Magic Kingdom, which led to thoughts of home.

Since I lost my parents last year, I find myself constantly second guessing who the *real me* is anymore. With no family left to speak of and most of my friends starting their own families, I was becoming a drifter without a true purpose in life. My only constant was an obsession with vampires. It kept me going when nothing else would.

I walked along the *Rue Legouvé*, through the *Passage des Marais*. Posters over posters lined the reddish walls. I squinted in the dim light to make out the advertisements on the curling and plastered papers but they were hidden amongst layers of graffiti. It looked as if they had been there for quite some time because many were faded, too. It's a shame because some would have probably been cool events to attend.

The sounds of the city faded the further in I traveled. Even the sirens I heard in the distance drifted away.

A rustling of old newspaper stopped me in my tracks. There was no wind blowing through this street. Turning around did me no good because no one was in sight to justify the sounds. I stopped and so did the noise. I walked a few more steps and it returned. At last, I turned around again and waited. Still, nothing came.

I turned the corner and sped up towards the Boulevard de Magenta, where my hotel lay only a few blocks beyond. Tall, black iron streetlights lined the boulevard, cascading light and shadows across my path. A shadow appeared behind me and disappeared just as fast. I turned again to look, to search, but there was no one in sight.

I told myself that it was just the exhaustion talking. It's nothing that a miracle shower head couldn't cure. I entered the hotel with a yawn and pushed my paranoia aside. The scent of cookies calmed me down. This time it was a macadamia nut cookie in my mouth when I stepped into the elevator.

***

The next afternoon, I walked the banks of Canal St. Martin. A small gift shop had its glass doors propped open, where a carousel of postcards stood calling out to me. It made me remember my promises to send them to several people back home.

Shelves of trinkets, jewelry, and stationery filled the tiny shop. An older woman stood behind the counter, drinking coffee and staring at nothing in particular. I spun the carousel back and forth and listened to it creak as I selected a few postcards and walked to the counter.

She smiled at me but said nothing. Maybe she didn't think I spoke French or maybe she just didn't want to talk. Either way, I also stayed silent so as not to interrupt her thoughts. She let the register tell me the total and I handed over my money. Even after she handed me my change and slid the postcards across the counter, she remained quiet. I forced a smile in her direction and left.

I sat on a bench overlooking the Canal. My pen was poised over the postcards as I tried to figure out what to say on each of them.

My phone rang and broke my concentration. It was Jen.

"Hey," I answered.

"Sorry I missed your call. I just got up and thought I'd give you a call. It's nine here...what time is it by you?"

I looked at my watch. "Three. I was just about to write you out a postcard." I tucked them into my purse and leaned back against the bench.

"So you left Romania early?"

"Ugh, don't remind me. It was really bad, Jen. I'm so pissed that I wasted all that money on the symposium. Transylvania itself was beautiful but I just couldn't stay there anymore."

"Was it because the symposium was bad or something else?"

A few birds landed on the bench behind me. I shooed them away. "Well, the symposium was filled with a mix of literature snobs and vampire fanatics."

"And you're both, so what was the problem?"

I rolled my eyes. "It wasn't like that. It just wasn't what I had expected. Then I met a guy named Alin."

"Okay, now we're getting somewhere. You guys do anything?"

I sighed. Where did I even begin? "He didn't turn out to be the guy I thought he was. He...." I didn't want to admit this to her. "He said he was a vampire and I believed him. It turns out he's in some weird cult where they drink the blood from farm animals."

There was silence on the other line for a long moment. "Was Chris right?"

It was my turn to be silent. Chris and I talked about vampires over the years and he always thought I was insane. After a while, I stopped mentioning it and gave up on the thought altogether. I think that's part of the reason why I'm so interested now. "What are you talking about?"

"I mentioned where you went and he said that you were probably looking for vampires."

I shook my head and lied. "No, I'm not. I'm learning about vampire myths and enjoying a long-needed vacation."

"If you say so. Still, you need to get over your vampire obsession and realize that there's going to be other men that won't break your heart like Chris did."

Ouch...she went there.

"You're quiet. You're thinking about him again, aren't you?"

"I hate that you know me so well."

She laughed. "That's why I'm your best friend, Dylan. So, you're in Paris now, right?"

"Yeah. I'll be here for a few more days, then a week in Florence and I'll be home."

"Okay. Call me more often. Don't leave me in the dark while you're out there, okay?"

I agreed and hung up.

As the evening pushed on, I took a leisurely walk around the Canal St. Martin, enjoying the nightlife. The sidewalks were covered with Sycamore trees that hung close to the path. I had thought Romania was full of dark corners but it was nothing compared to Paris. There were so many dimly lit streets as I went along that a sense of uneasiness soon washed over me.

The feeling of someone watching me started again. I stopped and looked around, turning in a circle to persuade my paranoia away. No…I was pretty sure that someone was watching me.

I squinted to read the street signs in desperate search for the one which would lead me back to the hotel.

"Dylan," a voice whispered in the darkness.

All of my worst fears crashed into me. *That couldn't be my name I just heard, Right?* I fought the urge to scream – scream anything. Should I ask who is there? Should I scream for help? I wasn't sure, but it wasn't a comfortable, friendly feeling coming across. There was no one visible on the street, no matter how hard I stared into the shadows behind me.

I stood still, waiting for a moment, but nothing happened. I turned slowly in wait, yet found the same results. There was nothing to be frightened of. It was late. I was still overtired. Rationalization was always my strong suit but nothing seemed to be working. Nonetheless, I decided not to stand here any longer. My pace quickened and I nearly tripped over myself in an effort to get to my hotel faster.

I kept glancing over my shoulder but nobody was following me. I just couldn't shake the suspicious feeling. I was almost at a full run now and glanced over my shoulder again when I suddenly slammed into someone. A loud "Oooph!" escaped my lips as I fell backwards onto the rough pavement. Apologies started before I even got to my feet.

It was one of the local police officers standing over me. He extended his hand to help me up. "*Êtes-vous bien?*"

"Yes, I'm fine," I replied with a shortness of breath. I brushed myself off and took a final glimpse behind me.

His eyes followed in suit as he tried to figure out what I was looking for. "Is someone bother you?" he asked in broken English.

"I…I'm not sure," I hesitated. "I didn't see anyone, but…." I made a dismissive hand gesture so I did not sound like an ignorant American tourist. "It's nothing." Besides, it's not like I was going to tell him that someone was calling my name when no one in this country even knew who I was.

The officer nodded. "*Bonsoir,*" he said and continued on his route.

Friendly, I thought. I wondered what he'd do if I had been in any real danger. It also occurred to me the French police should have known better English – but maybe, too, I should have known better French.

I walked the rest of the way to my hotel with the same uneasy feeling. I would have felt better if the police officer had walked back with me but he didn't offer and I didn't ask. Actually, I wasn't sure if my French vocabulary could have even handled it because his English sure as hell wouldn't have understood. He probably would have brought me to a McDonalds or something, if I were even that lucky.

I wasn't attacked on the way back, so I was feeling fortunate, despite the feeling of being stalked for the better part of the evening.

Once up in the safety of my room, I closed the curtains and made sure my door was locked. If there was someone out there, I wanted to feel safe. The deadbolt was secured, too. I eyed the small dresser and considered pushing it in front of the door but thought better of it. I zoomed through the hotel lobby so fast I didn't even see what flavors they had baked tonight. Damn it. My stomach growled at the thought and made me realize I skipped dinner.

The trip to the Canal stopped my night time sightseeing in Paris. For the next two days, I stuck to all the tourist traps and shopping centers. Each night, I was back in my hotel room by six, just before sunset. The days of taking chances like that were over. It pissed me off that I was frightened so easily but I reminded myself that it's a foreign country and things had to be a little different.

Someone had followed me, though. My imagination ran wild with possibilities. Did I think it was a vampire? Secretly, I sort of wished for it, but deep down I knew better. A vampire cult in Paris crossed my mind more than a few times. I highly doubted Alin's was the only cult like it in the world, but there was no way to be sure. With memories of Transylvania still fresh in my mind, I decided that it was time to leave Paris.

I ended my French expedition and made arrangements to take the train to Italy. Italian was the language I practiced more, so it was *Bonsoir* to the Parisian scene. I would be in Florence for a week and a half before I'd have to go back home. It was only supposed to be a week, I'd have more time now and hoped my experience there would be better.

Shannon Bell

Chapter 3

IT WAS TIME to call Jen again. I'd neglected to call her since Paris because of all of the sightseeing that's kept me busy.

Italy gave me some kind of purpose. Even if it only involved eating rustic Italian food and gazing at the amazing old architecture, it was a country which didn't need to re-invent itself over and over again like some of the countries in Europe. The history around every corner filled a part of my soul which France wasn't able to accomplish. The Italians were also friendlier, but it may have something to do with my Italian skills being better.

My hand hovered on the phone before I punched the numbers in.

"Dylan?" Jen sounded out of breath as she posed the question. "What the hell took you so long to call? I was ready to book a flight and find you."

I laughed. "Sorry, it's been hectic. I've changed my schedule a few times. I'm actually in Italy early."

"What'd you do that for?"

I wondered how much to tell her but it was Jen after all. "I got creeped out. Something scared me and I felt like I was being followed."

"Don't tell me you think it was a vampire." I swear she rolled her eyes over the phone. "I don't know what it is with you and vampires. You know they don't exist but it's like you're determined for someone to tell you one way or another."

"No, I don't think it was a vampire. But still, it was enough to make me want to leave Paris."

Jen was silent for a second. "You need to be careful. I really wish I came with you."

"You don't need to worry. I'm fine."

"I'm serious. I'll meet you in Italy by mid-week if you want. Then we can fly home together."

Tempting as it was, I wanted time to myself. "It's okay. My flight leaves in a week. There's still some sightseeing I want to do and then I'll be home. I promise."

"You better. What's the name of the hotel you're staying at?"

I told her and she wrote it down in case she had to

come track me down. I wasn't worried anymore. It'd been three days here and nothing has happened to me like it did in Paris.

"Are you at least having fun?"

"Yes, it's amazing. I wouldn't mind living here. People are always walking around, drinking coffee, eating gelato, and carrying on day and night. There's always something going on."

She sighed. "I really wish I came with you."

"Me, too. Listen, I signed up for a cooking class this evening so I need to get ready but I'll call you in a day or two, okay?"

We hung up after she swore she'd hop the next plane to Florence if I didn't call her by Tuesday. It was Sunday, which meant I still had plenty of time. Now it was on to learn how to cook risotto.

***

Between cooking classes, sightseeing, and drinking half-carafes of wine with every meal, the excitement of Florence was exhausting me. There were these little areas of the city telling different stories. Every block had a new mystery. I especially loved the area south of the Arno River, known as Oltrarno. Large buildings with immense iron doors were around every corner. Wondering what was behind those massive doors was part of the intrigue to Florence.

I slept in late today to have enough energy to go out exploring tonight. Room service was called up to my small room overlooking the Palazzo Pitti. After eating ravioli, I left the room with my messenger bag slung over my shoulder. It was supposed to be cold this evening. I decided to wear my favorite turquoise turtleneck over a pair of jeans. I'm five foot six and liked to look even taller, so my heeled boots were a natural choice. My tennis shoes peaked out at me and reminded me to be sensible, but fashion won. As I left the hotel, I promised myself not to stay out too late walking or my feet would pay for it later.

Couples bustled past me on the crowded streets of *Santo Spirito*. They were all headed back to the city center, towards the restaurants, bars, and over-priced, fancy hotels. It was where most of the tourists stayed because they didn't know any better. I, however, was headed in the opposite direction, where there were only little shops and quaint little trattorias on the outskirts of town. Most of my recent nights have been like this. Quiet walks gave me time to think in this beautiful city. Getting away from my job and my life in Florida was one of the best things I ever did. The change of pace helped me to become more free spirited, which is exactly what the vacation was all about.

The shops I passed now were small and piled one on top of each other along the road. Bookstores, pottery, jewelry, and wine shops all appeared to be family owned. Hand-written signs filled the thick paned windows. Some had flower pots in the front that made them inviting while others were barren. I found myself window shopping despite the late hour and the inability to see in them all that well.

I wandered the streets aimlessly. I had no responsibilities, alarm clocks for work, or drama to deal with. It was only me and the streets of Italy where I could walk, clear my head, and be at ease.

The lights were off in the stores and very few lamp posts were lit along the street. A few shop owners were locking up for the night and I was surprised to find that they stayed open as late as they did.

My mind told me to go back to Florida and hang out with Jen, my one friend who wasn't getting married. My heart told me it was the last thing I should actually do. Marriage was the opposite of what I wanted and the wedding invitations from all my friends were becoming irritating.

It was easily midnight and the streets had quieted significantly. The stone fountains that stood taller than me were gurgling loudly, though that was the only sound remaining in Oltrarno.

I turned down Borgo San Jacopo and passed a few

artisan shops closing up. A pudgy man in his late sixties locked the front door of a pottery shop as I strolled by.

I nodded to him. "*Buona Sera.*"

He stepped into my path. "Are you lost?"

I smiled at him. "No, just headed back to my hotel."

The old man nodded. "It's late. A woman of your beauty should not be out this late."

I nodded in understanding and watched him go back into his shop where he sat at the counter working on piles of paperwork.

Florence was a confusing city to walk around at night. Rather than placing street signs at every intersection, the names were printed on small metal placards placed on the side of buildings at every corner. It turned navigation into a game of hide and seek, though I was the one searching. There wasn't enough light to read the signs. Figuring out where I needed to make my next turn was time consuming.

I turned the corner onto *via Barbadori* and saw no familiar signs of civilization. This isn't where I was supposed to be. The name didn't sound familiar but I was hoping it would get me back to the main road where my hotel was.

There was a street lamp at the end of the road…or alley as it was. I reached for the map in my messenger bag blindly and stumbled on something. I caught my balance and took a few more steps forward.

It was now that I wished I had asked the shop owner for directions. The single street lamp acted as a beacon. With map in hand, I started towards it to figure out how to get out of here.

A loud noise crashed behind me and I stumbled again. My boot heel caught in the pavement cracks but I saved myself from falling and stepped towards the sound to investigate. It was the old man throwing garbage out at the far end of the alley. I caught my breath and watched him as he disappeared. Realizing it was a dead end, I turned on my heel to go back in the right direction.

Tripping on the same divot in the road, I wasn't able to catch my balance this time. A hand caught me around the shoulder. The height was all wrong to be the old man. Before I could let out a scream, someone covered my mouth. My elbows jabbed into the body behind me to no avail, but the person made no sound. It was as if my elbows were meeting stone instead of flesh.

Thankful I was wearing my heeled boots, I was able to use used the three inches to make contact with my attacker's foot. The stomp was a little more effective judging from the Italian curses that were muttered behind me. Before I could get another jab or kick in, the hand around my collarbone tightened and dragged me several feet down the alley, closer to the streetlight. He pushed me against the stone wall and took a step back with his other hand still planted firmly across my mouth.

"You're certainly a fighter," the man spoke. In the light, I could tell that the man standing in front of me was attractive with a strong jaw line. His shirt was taut against his chest and there was a slight amusement behind his blue eyes.

I cursed at him but it came out as mumbles thanks to the placement of his hand. His gaze burned into me as he took another step towards me and rested one hand nonchalantly on the brick wall above me.

"I'm going to remove my hand and you're not going to scream, okay?"

I nodded and swallowed hard.

His hand slowly slipped away from my mouth and slid down my neck. His fingertips grazed my skin and came to a rest on my shoulder.

I knew screaming would do me no good. His solid frame loomed over me by six inches. My previous self-defense techniques had been useless against him. I opted for reasoning with the handsome attacker in front of me. "What do you want from me?"

"No. What do you want from *me*?"

"What?"

"Why have you been looking for us?"

I stared at him, wondering who he had me confused

with. "Looking for who?"

It was late and I just wanted to find my hotel. The sooner we could clear this up, the sooner I could be on my way.

He shook his head slowly. "Don't play coy."

What the hell was he talking about? His gaze met mine and his set jaw gave no indication of moving anytime soon.

"You know what I am, Dylan."

I went rigid when he said my name. Panic set in all over again. I squirmed under his grip. "What do you want from me?"

"Look at me and answer my question."

Before I could ask anything else from him, I saw what he wanted me to see. He smiled at me, showing two elongated incisors behind his lips.

One word screamed through my mind. *Vampire*.

"Correct."

No.

"Why are you so quick to deny what's standing in front of you? You seek the truth. Here I am." He stepped back as if to make a demonstration of who—or rather, what—he was.

I simply stared and took in what stood before me. Designer jeans, a button down shirt, and a stunning face surrounded by short and tousled, black hair. It's not what I had ever imagined, though somehow it seemed to fit now. My heart pounded a little faster as I realized that a vampire was standing in front of me.

My mouth went dry. I had questions to ask and couldn't seem to formulate words.

He stepped in even more intimately to me and kept me pinned to the wall while one muscular arm hovered beside me.

I gulped hard, making a sound which seemed to echo out of my body.

Could he hear that?

"Yes."

"I'm sorry?"

He chuckled softly. "I could hear you swallow. It is what you were wondering, yes?"

"Oh."

Oh. My. God. I was going to die.

I continued to stare, trying to get past my shock and the giant knot now swelling at the base of my throat. I closed my eyes for a moment to try and gather my thoughts.

"Are you ready to answer my question now?"

What was I supposed to tell him? *Ha, well I was only wondering if you guys were real and you are, so have a nice eternity.* I glanced up at him to see an amused look on his face. Dimples formed on either side of his mouth.

Shit. He was reading my thoughts again. My palms began to sweat and panic set in when the sound of his laughter filled the alley.

This is great. I have to stand here while a vampire of all things laughed at me. I thought back on the night in Paris. I never actually saw anyone, but now it made me question if my gut feeling was correct.

He abruptly stopped laughing. "Dylan, let me ask again. Why have you been hunting for vampires?"

My shoulder was rubbing against his fingers but I couldn't move. The touch of his cold fingers left goose bumps across my skin and me slightly breathless. "I was…" I couldn't think of the right word to explain my curiosity. The whole idea sounded insane when it came down to it. "I wouldn't really call it hunting-"

"Listen, your mind is an open book." He blinked and shifted his eyes to take the whole view of me in. I shifted awkwardly under his scrutiny. "You've come alone, have you not?"

"Yes," I cursed myself for telling him the truth. I swallowed again, wondering if I was going to die tonight. I shouldn't have told him I was alone.

"Did anyone know you were looking for vampires?"

"No." I opted for some honesty here, hoping my life

would be spared. "But I wasn't really looking for vampires. I was simply curious about your existence." It sounded lame, even to me.

"And now what?"

"I don't know. I never thought I would ever come face to face with one, so…"

He laughed softly to himself. "Well, you've found one."

I nodded, unable to speak.

"What made you decide to come here to look?" He inched into my personal space and inhaled something in the air around me.

I held my breath as he sniffed my skin. His face was so close to mine that my whole body tensed. Part of me was hoping he'd ravage me against the wall and the other part was waiting to feel the pressure of his fangs against my throat.

"I wasn't looking," I protested again, swallowing as his fingers danced along my neckline. "I went to Romania for a symposium, then Paris and then here. They…they were just places I wanted to see." I slowly let out my breath as he continued to inch even closer, exploring my neck.

He seemed to think about this for a few moments. "And your fascination with vampires?"

Was I really having a conversation with the undead? He seemed very human. I shrugged in response. "It's been going on since I was a child." Why did I keep talking? My mind slowly replayed the whole story of Alin and I realized that the man before me was very different from the cult in Brasov.

"Alin was a fool."

Hearing his voice snapped me back into reality and I stared at the figure who had me pressed against the brick wall. My eyes widened as I realized he probably heard the whole story of Transylvania inside my head.

He wasn't going to chastise me like Alin did. He already admitted to being the real deal.

"Do *I* scare you?" He asked, leaning his strong body into me, grinning slightly as his fangs peeked out under his upper lip.

I nodded and whispered, "Yes."

"Good."

I looked down while his muscular build pressed into me ever so slightly. He continued to laugh softly. I breathed in, trying to calm myself. The body in front of me smelled. Not a bad smell, but it was familiar, like honeysuckle perhaps. It was intoxicating, even under these circumstances.

He suddenly turned on me and became very serious.

"Don't," he whispered.

I stared at him. He touched the collar of my turtleneck, sending goose bumps across my entire body. I was suddenly sure of only one thing: I was going to die tonight.

"Don't what?" I asked, wondering if fate should be tempted by asking questions.

He positioned himself where his eyes were level with mine. They were the deepest blue I had ever seen. "Don't think that covering your neck with this flimsy cloth will stop me from seeking the blood that's pounding through your veins right now," he whispered.

I tried to keep my heart from racing and reminded myself that he was about to drain me.

There was no response to give him. My mind continued to spin out of control and I couldn't focus on anything but him. He was a God who oozed sex appeal, yet I was going to die by his hand in an alley. This was not how I had pictured my death. I imagined living a full life and dying of old age. Something resonated in me and realized that up until this point I didn't really believe in vampires. Wrong again.

I was going to die tonight and wouldn't have even known my killer's name.

"It's Niccolò."

I inhaled sharply. He actually answered me!

Niccolò pulled the turtleneck down more and exposed my neck. He bent down and licked a small area of my throat. I felt his fangs graze my skin.

"Are you prepared to die tonight?" His breath caressed my skin like velvet.

My eyes widened at him in response because my voice failed me. I felt my heartbeat speed up to a deafening rate. All I could hear was the blood pounding in my ears. A bead of sweat began to slide down my forehead despite the cool temperature in the alley.

"The more you panic, the closer your blood gets to the surface," he announced, adding a chill across my skin. "That makes it much easier for me."

I swallowed hard again and focused on breathing. *In, out, in, out.* I closed my eyes for a moment to decide if I should say anything to him. I was confident that arguing or begging would get me nowhere. Each breath I took was getting shakier and the thoughts of passing out in the next few seconds occurred to me. Fainting would be the worst thing that could happen right now. Begging for my life would be difficult if I was unconscious.

Niccolò didn't let me forget he was there. His fangs continued to press against my skin, not quite breaking the surface. I wasn't sure what he was waiting for, unless he was expecting me to start screaming. We'd be waiting for a while because no matter how much I wanted to, I knew nothing would come out. Whenever I was really scared, my voice failed me. It wasn't a very good survival tactic, but there it was. I wasn't sure if there was anything to say at this point. I was hoping it would be quick and painless. I couldn't get the idea out of my head that I'd be left in an alley for the Italian police to find. They probably wouldn't even try to identify me or call anyone because I was a tourist. Was a Jane Doe still a Jane Doe in Italy?

Something or someone made a sound at the other end of the alley. A dumpster lid flew open or a box was thrown around, causing a loud crash to reverberate through the alley. I glanced at the sound and felt Niccolò pause. I let out a soft gasp when I realized that it was the old man from the pottery store.

Before I could scream, several things happened. He pressed himself down the front of me, sandwiching me between his hard body and the equally hard brick wall. Then the vampire's mouth descended onto mine, kissing me with a crushing intensity lasting for at least half a minute. Somewhere during the kiss, I rose up on my toes to meet his lips.

The commotion at the other end of the alley stopped. He withdrew from the kiss as quickly as it had begun. I watched him take a step back and lick his lips to savor the taste. I backed myself against the wall to steady myself and pressed my palms flat against the cold brick. The kiss left me breathless. Not because it was from a vampire, but because it was powerful. No one's ever kissed me like that. If Chris had, I might have fought to stay with him.

I fought the urge to run my fingers through his short waves and press my lips against his again. I also fought the urge to turn and run in the opposite direction because I was attracted to a vampire.

"That was not meant to happen." He looked past me, purposefully avoiding my gaze.

I took in a very shaky breath. *What was that?*

"The shop owner you saw earlier hadn't seen you walk past again. He was checking to see if you were okay. He would have called the police if he thought you were in danger. It was the only way to be convincing." Niccoló looked away as he didn't believe what he was saying, either.

"Oh," was all I could manage out. I couldn't get my mind to make any coherent thoughts. It made sense he didn't want to get caught, but a kiss? I wasn't complaining, which should have meant that I was completely insane.

Normal people don't want to be kissed by a vampire who's about to kill them!

"You are one of the strangest mortals I've ever met."

I needed to get better at keeping my thoughts to myself. The fact he could read my mind was getting annoying and more than a little embarrassing.

"You're one of the strangest vampires I've ever met."

I countered.

He laughed again. "I'm the *only* vampire you've ever met."

"True," I hesitated. "But how can you want to kill me in one moment and kiss me the next?" I probably should have kept my mouth shut. I didn't want to remind him of his original plan.

"I don't have a response for you. We couldn't get caught, and, your skin felt so warm...." He trailed off. "You're different somehow."

"Thanks, I think." I decided to push my luck. "How...how am I different?"

Niccolò paused to deliberate over an answer. There was silence for what seemed like several minutes while I leaned against the wall and waited for him to answer me. "I haven't kissed a mortal on the mouth since I was one myself," he spoke matter-of-factly. "The only kisses are ones which bring their death and thus my survival." Once again he was quiet for a few moments before speaking again. "The taste of your mouth was exhilarating," he confessed.

My cheeks flushed no matter how hard I worked at getting them not to. "But how is it you can do that without wanting to...."

"I fed a few minutes before finding you. As long as I feed at least once every two or three days, then anything else is merely sport." He looked at me curiously, taking a step forward. "Unless you were offering yourself up?" His eyebrows arched, waiting for an invitation.

"Me? No." I thought about what he said. "I was going to be *sport* for you?" Should I be insulted or terrified? My life almost ended at the hands of a vampire.

"You sound upset." He seemed amused. "Would you have rather been a meal than recreation?"

"Well, I don't know. I guess both would end the same way," I said. Since he seemed willing to answer a few questions, I kept at it. "Why did you think I was looking for vampires?"

"You attended the vampire symposium as part of the Transylvanian Society for Dracula. We keep an eye on attendees every year. We are able to know where everyone is headed thanks to people on the inside. When you didn't return to Florida, you were a target to watch."

My mouth dropped. "I went on vacation afterwards."

He leaned his arm forward and tapped his cold finger directly on my temple. "Open book, remember? You crossed my path two days ago when you were having dinner at the little bistro on Portinari. You were thinking about vampires and if any were around the city."

"I also remember laughing about those ideas. How did you know I was serious?"

Niccolò smiled at me. "You looked very determined. And you are a truth seeker."

Truth seeker. That's the second time I've been called that. Is that what I was?

"Hmmm." I yawned involuntarily. I was beginning to feel the time now that I was in no immediate danger. At the very least I hoped to be right about the danger aspect.

"You're tired. Would you like me to walk you back to your hotel?"

I hesitated, not knowing what to say. A vampire wanted to walk with me? I was thoroughly confused. First, he drags me into an alley where I think he's going to kill me. Then he kisses me. And now he wants to escort me back to my hotel? This was too much for one night.

"Okay," I agreed, trying not to sound as dumbfounded as I felt. I did need a little more confirmation in order to be able to sleep tonight. "You're letting me live?"

"For now."

Comforting.

He shrugged. A simple gesture told me he didn't know what else to say. "I am not always the one to make final decisions."

Niccolò led me out of the alley and back onto the cobblestone road. No shops were open. Fountains gurgled and loose pebbles clicked under my heels. Otherwise, everything had a deafening silence to it. Streetlights at various corners illuminated small patches of our way down the narrow road. Bicycles were parked along the path and we weaved around them to continue past. I stole a few glances at him in an effort to read something out of his expressionless face. I kept up with his pace and let my hands rest in my back pockets.

I didn't know what to say to or ask of him. There were many things I wanted to know, but I had no idea where to begin or what my limitations were. It was a thin, imaginary line drawn that I didn't want to cross. Anything I could say or do could upset him and make me his next meal. As I glanced sideways at him, though, I wasn't so sure. He was more human than any previous ideas I had about vampires. He stopped when we reached the small hotel I was staying at. Of course he knew where I was staying....

I looked at him again. I mean, I really looked at him. *Will I see you again?* The idea of getting to know him seemed like part of my destiny that had to be fulfilled. I couldn't go home to Florida without getting some questions answered. The regret would be too much. He *was* a vampire, after all.

"Do you want to see me again?" He asked softly. He reached towards me and pushed a strand of hair behind my ear.

I shivered slightly and nodded. It was an easy

response, though it shouldn't have been. I watched how casually he leaned against the stone wall and eerie part of my body screamed with a different reaction. I wanted to get to know him and learn everything about him and run screaming in the opposite direction at the same time.

"There's a small *trattoria* on *Vellutini*," he teased into my ear. "I will meet you there at eight tomorrow."

Before I could agree, he was gone. There was no sign of him down the road as if he vanished out of thin air. I rubbed my arms and let out a deep breath. I walked into the hotel slightly wide-eyed and made my way up to my room.

I needed to make sense of everything that transpired, though I couldn't get a grasp on any of it. First vampires existed, then they didn't, and now they do again. Without a doubt, they exist.

Niccolò was absolutely terrifying, yet in a heart-stopping, exhilarating sort of way. He was attractive in every sense of the word and he made me weak in the knees at the very thought of him. The way he could read every single thought which was in my head was more than nerve-wracking. Most importantly, he was a vampire. He was an actual immortal, blood-drinking vampire who let me live.

Every part of me throbbed with an intensity that craved his touch. My head hit the pillow but sleep was the last thing on my mind.

Chapter 4

I WOKE LATE in the morning uncertain if everything I went through last night was real. The smarter part of my mind convinced me that it was all a dream. If that was the case, why did my turtleneck smell like honeysuckle? No, Niccolò was real. I was also sure he wasn't going to kill me – not yet, anyways.

My trip was almost over. Five days from now, I was supposed to get on a plane and leave all this behind. As it was right now, there was no way that was going to happen. Leave Niccolò, the very thing that had always kept me going? I needed more time.

The airlines could move my flight. More time in Italy…that's exactly what I needed. I had to find out more about Niccolò.

My stomach growled and it took me a few minutes to remember the last time I had eaten anything. It was almost noon. I was meeting Niccolò at eight. He might not show up, but I wanted to make sure to be at the bistro on time regardless.

***

The massive stone bridge stood before me and beckoned me to cross it. With my messenger bag slid over my shoulders, I started weaving in and out of the pedestrian traffic standing around it. The jewelry shops fought to take over the entire path and the sales people were pushy with their strands of gold in my face and requests for me to step inside. I ignored them and finally made it into South Centro, near Tornabuoni, where the buildings stood tall with all its posh clothing stores.

Mannequins stood behind the glass windows in all the latest fashions. Some were too short for my liking and others were too daring. Then a black skirt caught my eye and called out to me. I was going broke and getting tired of the same outfits in my suitcase.

The prices were high. Without even going inside, I knew that they were more than what I could afford. I still had a little money left, and even though I knew I shouldn't, I couldn't resist the urge to go inside to see what mysteries the stores held.

Leather and lace. Tempting...so very tempting. Every rack had a different combination of black leather, white leather, black lace.... The European sizes had me lost so I held a few up to my figure in the mirror to my right and took a few to try on. A sales clerk was in the back but it sounded like she was fighting with a boyfriend on the phone and I didn't want to interrupt.

A black leather skirt hugged my hips as I stared at my reflection. The slit in the back was daring but not slutty. The tag almost gave me a heart attack but it had been a while since I'd splurged on anything for myself. I thought of meeting Niccoló later. Would he like the skirt? Would he notice? Before I could think of anything else, the skirt was in my hand and my credit card was being swiped for the purchase.

I headed out the open glass doors and stepped onto the curb. A large tour bus with tourists hanging themselves out the windows to take photos of the famous shopping district and the stone statue that stood to my left was stopped at the light. I crossed to the other side after it passed in search of a place to grab a quick slice of pizza.

A small restaurant and bar was around the corner, appropriately named Yankee Bar. I'd heard about it in passing from other tourists. It was one of the few American bars around where you could order a drink in English without having to worry about whether the bartender understood you or not. The bar wasn't what caught my attention. It was the sign on the dark wooden door about a bartender. They were hiring. I contemplated going in to make an inquiry. After all, managing a bar qualified me. Getting a job here would solve so many problems. More money meant more time…and possibly some more outfits, too.

"Can I help you?" A twenty-something blonde man came to the door. His blond spiky hair was a contrast against his wire frame glasses and small build. I must have stood there a little too long since he noticed me. His American accent was welcoming.

I nodded towards the help wanted sign.

"You bartend?"

"I used to. Now I manage a restaurant back in the States. What kind of money are the bartenders making here?" It certainly wouldn't hurt to find out a little information.

"Ahh, you're American! Great! The clientele is a bunch of tourists and they tip really well. Most of the crowd is a bunch of trust-fund kids who travel around Europe on mom and dad's money, so—"

"Citizenship's not an issue?" My eyebrows rose in question, wondering if that would be the thing to hold me back.

He reached into his pocket and pulled out a business card. "My name's Matt. Why don't you stop by on Thursday and we can talk about that and some other details then?"

I took the card and slid it into my back pocked before I extended my hand. "I'm Dylan. And yeah, I think I'll see you Thursday. Thanks again."

"See you Thursday," Matt commented, closing the door to the bar.

I wasn't sure what my plan was, but I felt like I was getting closer to having one. I was convinced that if I could land a job bartending, I could stay in Italy longer. Plus, I still couldn't get the idea of having some more clothes available to me. Back home I was a huge clothes junkie and living out of a suitcase with limited possibilities was putting a huge damper on my style.

The leather skirt in the fancy boutique bag hung from my wrist as I continued down the street.

I got back to the room around six and hopped into a shower. The hotel-supplied shampoo smelled like lavender and invigorated my senses as it worked into a lather on the top of my head. I grabbed my razor and managed an awkward pose in the shower to ensure that every inch of stubble was removed. Not that I expected anything other than conversation, but it still had to be done.

I grabbed a towel and twisted my hair up to give it a chance to dry naturally before I took a hairdryer to it. The few steps over to my bed assured me that my outfit was ready to go. The black skirt laid there just waiting to be worn.

The window across the room showed me that it was still light out. The sun was just starting to drop. Would Niccolò be up yet? Would it be rude to even ask?

I managed into black panties and zipped up the black skirt that ran the better part of my left side. A black and burgundy print top hung off one shoulder and I stared down at my naked feet. Neither black boots, sneakers, nor brown sandals were good options. The brown sandals would clash, the sneakers would make me look like a tourist, and the black boots would make me appear as if I wanted more than conversation from him.

The bartending job was looking better and better because I could go back and get those cute strappy black heels that the mannequin was wearing back on Tornabuoni.

I spent too damn much on the skirt not to wear it so I zipped the boots up the length of my calves before another moment's hesitation.

There wasn't much time before I had to go meet Niccolò. I was only vaguely aware of where the street was but my map hadn't let me down yet. It was in South Centro, though, so I would need time to cross the Ponte S. Trinita

Bridge.

By the time I crossed the front of Palazzo Pitti, the boots were killing me. The glances I was getting from some of the local men told me I looked good, though, so it kept me moving forward.

A gelato shop at the base of the bridge was packed. I crossed the narrow street to the other side to avoid the line. The bridge itself had a small walking path where a few others walked, headphones crammed in their ears. Cars were parked in rush hour traffic on the bridge while their drivers honked their horns and waved their hands. A few scooters daringly maneuvered through the traffic and continued on their way.

The piazza was to my left and the next road was supposed to be Vellutini. Instead, I stared at a small stone church, dilapidated from centuries of abuse. The small placard embedded in the stone told me I was at Parione, not Vellutini. These road names were so frustrating.

The night sky was getting darker and was already streaked with shades of red and pink. The lampposts were cascading shadows across the sidewalks. I stood under one to see a little better and held the little pop-up map in my hand so I could trace the roads and figure out the *trattoria* I was supposed to meet Niccolò at.

My foot incessantly tapped the concrete where I stood. I turned the map every possible way but the name of the road was not listed on this damned map. I tried to look it up in my phone, but that was no help, either. Would he leave if I didn't get there right away? I was hoping not. I glanced at my watch and noticed it was 8:10. Damn it! All the road names seemed to be different deviations of the same word. *Bellatini. Bellalago. Vell...* I should have asked him for a landmark or something before just eagerly agreeing to the place he told me.

Couples bustled past me but none slowed down. They were probably tourists, too, so they wouldn't know where it was any better than I did.

A little gelato shop was at the corner from where I stood. It was one of the few I hadn't been to yet and I was contemplating going over if I couldn't find the road soon.

"Ciao," a voice whispered.

I looked up. "Niccolò," I whispered in shock that he really showed up. It wasn't until this moment that I realized I was convinced I'd never see him again. "Hi."

"Lost, *mia mortale?*" He asked with a grin. *My mortal one.*

"I couldn't find the street." My frustration subsided as I folded my map and shoved it in my purse. I looked back up at him, fascinated by the sparkle in his eyes. "I'll follow you."

"Sure. I was late as well. And please, it's Nico."

I looked up to question, but he took me by the hand and led the way. I was surprised at the strength in his hand. It was like being able to squeeze a statue, as if it was made of a not so pliable clay. I was holding hands with a vampire in the middle of a crowded street and no one seemed to notice.

I didn't understand how this could happen. How could people not notice?

"Nico?" I was hoping he could shed some light on this for me.

"Not now," he calmly replied. "Wait until we're completely alone and then you can ask your questions." He walked into the crowded restaurant with me at his side.

Completely alone...*right*.

I nodded while he held the door to the *trattoria* open.

The *trattoria* was a very quaint family operation on a busy corner across from a fancy hotel. A menu board stood outside, where today's special was the four cheese ravioli and pasta fagioli. Couples going in and out of the place kept the small dining room perpetually full. Small was an understatement; there might have had fifteen tables total, all of which were spread between two different rooms and separated by a wood burning oven.

He seated us at a table in the darkest corner of the smallest room. "I don't actually scare you, do I?"

"Yes and no. Yesterday in the alley, you scared the

shit out of me. I was convinced you were going to kill me. Then there was the…." My cheeks flushed. "Now, though, not as much."

I was not sure if I should have said that last part. Maybe he wanted to make sure that I was scared all the time.

Niccolò pushed the menu at me. "Are you hungry?"

"A little." I eyed him cautiously before asking, "Are *you* hungry?"

"Dylan, Dylan, Dylan," he whispered, as if toying with me. "I haven't been hungry for anything on a menu in a very long time."

"Right," I said dryly while paging through the menu aimlessly. Of course not - I knew that. I made a mental check mark next to my ever-growing list of questions that I would ask if given the chance.

A petite waitress with her dark hair pulled up into a knot on the top of her head came over to the table. She told us the specials and seemed to bounce in place with all of her pent up energy. I looked up from the menu and ordered in my bastardized Italian. Nico said a few more things to her before she nodded and disappeared. I raised an eyebrow and wondered if he was going to translate what he just said to her.

"I was apologizing for your poor Italian. Where did you learn to speak like that?"

My face burned with embarrassment. "Audio CDs."

He started laughing. "Do me a favor, will you?"

I looked up at him, waiting.

"Get your money back," he said, laughing again. He had a thick, rich laugh that was warm and inviting. The sound alone played along the hairs on my arm.

I couldn't get over this. No one seemed to notice that he was a vampire. They treated him just as they treated me. Could people not see the difference? His skin was a paler shade of the olive skinned people surrounding the restaurant. His eyes were a true blue, not the muted shades everyone else seemed to have, and had a sparkle that made me wonder if I had ever understood what blue *was* until I looked into them. Other than that, though, it *was* hard to tell. Although he could actually pull it off, I knew the truth and could never look at him the same as everyone else.

"Dylan?"

I snapped out of my daze and looked up at him. "Yes?"

"Calm down. Your mind is spinning out of control and it's hard to decipher everything. You will have your chance to ask questions, I promise. Everything will be fine."

I nodded, not trusting my voice. *Everything is fine. Just having dinner with a vampire, that's all.* I reached over and broke off a piece of bread from the basket on the table to pop it in my mouth.

He smiled as my head cleared enough for him to read my thoughts. This was a convenient way to communicate, I had to admit. Dangerous, but convenient. I just had to watch what I was thinking about, which was harder than imaginable.

As dinner, or more appropriately, *my* dinner, arrived, I glanced over at him when I could smell the amount of garlic permeating from my dish. I raised an eyebrow at him and he chuckled.

"Have as much as you like."

"Really?"

"If it bothered me, I'd have to move to a different country. Old wives' tale."

It made me wonder what other speculations I'd read over the years were just old wives' tales. As my plate of pasta sat in front of me, I realized how hungry I actually was and started eating, acutely aware that the man across from me was watching every bite I took.

We left the restaurant and as we headed down the street, he guided me in the direction he wanted us to walk.

"Have you been to the Giardino di Boboli yet?"

I shook my head. "Not yet."

"We'll head that way. It's my favorite spot in all of Italy."

We entered the Boboli Gardens through an entrance just past Palazzo Pitti. My heart was beating recklessly fast as

I hesitated blurting out all my questions at once. We walked past one couple as they headed to the exit and then we were alone. Shrubs surrounded our path and an ornate stone fountain gurgled water in front of us. It was the only sound to be heard.

The gardens were dimly lit, the most light concentrated around the statues throughout. A few birds chirped in the distance and the air grew a little cooler as the wind blew from the Northeast. We walked into the large expanse of the gardens, where several different paths stemmed off from where we stood. Tall cypress trees lined the paths and carved out the walkway we chose. Closer to us were perfectly geometric shrubs. Greenery was everywhere around us as we ascended a large hill which, as we continued to climb it, was taking the breath out of me.

We reached the top of the hill where I walked around, looked at the statues and tried to make out the building in the background, Fort Belvedere. Nico stood quiet, taking in the view of the gardens, seeming to focus on things I could not see. He turned to me after a moment. "I used to come here as a mortal, too. It was my mother's favorite place as well."

"Really?" I asked in shock that he was sharing personal details without being asked, especially of his mortal life. We sat on a small cement bench in view of a greenish body of water, a retention pond of sorts with a beautiful fountain of Neptune in the middle.

He was silent for a moment. "I don't think I've actually ever told anyone that before. She loved the gardens so much, it's how she named me. The man who designed the gardens was named Niccolò Tribolo. The gardens were for the wife of the grand duke of Tuscany, one of the Medici men."

I smiled at him, getting a strong sense of humanity about him and enjoying hearing about his history and human life. Just when I was about to ask how he ended up with this fate, he let out an audible sigh and shook his head as if to push those memories out of his head.

"On to you. You have questions." He made it a statement, as though he could see my mind trying to form sense of my thousands of questions.

I nodded.

"Okay," he said with a grin. "Ask."

"Really?" I took a seat on the edge of the bench across from a huge statue, which looked like the head of Michelangelo's David.

"I might not answer them, but you can certainly ask." He leaned against the statue and watched me.

I smiled back and looked around to make sure we were alone, "All right. Well, how long have you been a vampire?"

He laughed at my secrecy. "A very long time. I was turned into what I am now back in 1747, in Firenze, err Florence, just after the reign of the Medici family. I was thirty and will forever be so." He made this into an equal questioning. "And you, Dylan, how old are you?"

I stared at him curiously for a moment before answering. "Twenty-eight." I thought about what he'd said. He's been a vampire longer than the United States has been a country. The knowledge of that seemed overwhelming. "Wait, how did you not know how old I was? You seem to know everything else!"

He smiled. "I only know if you think about it."

"Oh." I thought about my next question, wondering how many he was going to let me ask. "Can you go out in the daylight?"

He shook his head. "No. I haven't seen a sunrise since I was mortal, though I still remember what it looks like. It was bright pink. Funny how it works," he commented, recollecting. "You have more questions, don't you?"

I nodded. I felt like I was interviewing him or something. I did change my flights just so I could have this opportunity, though, so I went for it. "What about sleeping? Do you sleep?"

He stretched out his arms and let out a theatrical yawn. "Yes, during the day. And no, not in a coffin. But I don't dream," he added.

"Really?"

"Which part surprises you? Is it that I don't sleep in a coffin or that I don't dream?"

I thought about it for a minute. "Both, I guess. I can't imagine not dreaming, though. I mean, it's weird."

He laughed out loud this time. "Not dreaming is the weird thing about tonight? Dylan, you amaze me."

I stared at him, not knowing what to say.

"You've got to get these vampire stereotypes out of your head. I've read the books and seen the movies, too. Hollywood's got it all wrong."

"They do?" I asked. "Like what?

"Well, I can tell you I certainly don't sparkle if I go out in the sun," he commented while rolling his eyes.

It made me laugh because I knew which movie he was referring to. "No, I didn't think that you would. So then tell me, where *do* you sleep?"

"Out there. Come." Nico turned suddenly, putting his arm around me. He led me out of the gardens and kept his gaze focused straight ahead as we walked at a brisk pace up the stairs of Palazzo Pitti.

I looked at him, not sure if I should be scared or not. We reached the top and overlooked the greater part of Oltrarno and he pointed at nothing in particular, though the sight was breathtaking. To think my hotel was just minutes from here and I hadn't seen any of this yet.

"Everywhere. Nowhere." He pointed at the whole city and took a seat on the edge of the roof.

"You realize that you, in no way, answered my question," I remarked defiantly, sitting next to him, extremely aware my shoulder was touching his.

He struggled with his next answer, making a few faces before he decided what to say. "I can't tell you *exactly* where I sleep. It would be too dangerous for both of us."

"Hmmm."

He looked over at me, apologizing with his eyes. He knew it wasn't the answer I was looking for. Nico watched me for several minutes without saying a word. I held his gaze, not wanting to be the first to turn away.

"Nico."

He blinked, waiting for me to say what was on my mind. His expression clearly showed he wanted to know where my mind was headed.

"What is this?" It sounded strange, even to me. It was something had been bothering me since we had arrived at the Boboli Gardens and I needed to convince myself without a shadow of a doubt that he wasn't going to kill me.

"I'm not sure I understand the question," he said, his eyes focusing on me.

"This, what we're doing here. I just need to figure things out in my head from yesterday. You aren't trying to…well…so are we like…friends?" I hesitated on the last words, not wanting to jump to conclusions. Not wanting to sound like a high school girl either, I quickly added, "I just want to make sure you've decided not to kill me."

His lips quivered and I knew he was holding back a laugh as he brushed my cheek with his index finger and leaned in to me. My heart stopped beating. "We can be friends," he breathed, his lips intensely intimate along my neck. His lips hesitated over my throat. "Or we can be more."

My nerves kicked into high gear. More? More what? I had to keep reminding myself of what he was. I also had to remind myself to inhale and exhale. He was playing with my emotions. One moment he was charming and the next, well, that was the question. I fought internally with how to respond. I wasn't even sure if I *could* respond with his mouth so close to me.

"Dylan?" he asked, his breath cold on my skin.

I couldn't think straight. He could take me right here and I wouldn't fight him. He could have me and I think I would die with a smile on my face.

"Dylan? Are you okay?"

He pressed his lips to the base of my throat and kissed me, letting his lips linger. They were cold and moist and completely intoxicating. I didn't want to say anything. I just wanted him to continue with what he was doing.

His lips slid in an upward trail on my neck, planting a small kiss every so often until he reached my ear. I knew he could tell my heart was racing. He kissed right below my earlobe and sent chills across my entire body.

"We could do this all night, if you wish. I struggled for a response, completely convinced that I was going to faint in the next few moments if I couldn't get some oxygen to my brain.

I gasped and took in enough air to function. I pressed the palms of my hands against his chest and pushed slightly to distance our bodies for a moment so I could think straight. I couldn't budge him unless he wanted to move, but luckily he got the hint. He backed up and watched me with an intense gaze.

I swallowed hard, hoping to gain my voice back. As much as I wanted him to do whatever he wanted to do to me right now, I needed answers. I needed to make sure he wasn't going to get carried away and kill me. "What is going through your head right now?" I asked. It was a fair question, since he could read my mind so easily.

"It wasn't obvious?" he chuckled.

I looked at him in hopes that he would give me a more concrete answer. "Seriously. I mean, how are you attracted to me?"

I couldn't figure out why this gorgeous creature was interested in me. I had my flaws for sure as I thought about my own physique against his. I had an athletic build with a little meat that gave me some healthy curves. Nico, on the other hand, was lean and muscular, and on an entirely different level of hotness than I was.

"It's been a long time since I felt the warmth of a mortal. And you -." His gaze roamed the length of me...you are so beautiful and so warm." He saw right through me, reading through my own insecurities. "Being honest about myself would be a deal breaker with anyone, cold-blooded killer and all. Even so, you know what I am and you are still sitting beside me."

"But," I interrupted. "How *can* you be around me? What's different between me and your," I almost didn't want to say it, "victims?"

He reached out to me and took one of my hands. "During that night in the alley, the plan was to kill you. I heard the shop owner coming and something changed inside me. Not only could I not let him see who I was but also I knew that I couldn't risk hurting you, either. As I said the other night, you're different."

"Oh." It was a lame response but it was all I could seem to manage. This was not at all how I imagined my trip going and would never look at my life the same again. I was falling for a vampire. I was terrified of that part of him, but the rest – he was unlike anyone else I've ever met – even after omitting the whole blood-drinking, immortal aspects. Nico was different, like he had said about me.

Things definitely couldn't get any stranger, then something hit me with what he had just said. "What do you mean that the *plan* was to kill me?" My voice became a little louder than it should have.

Nico got up and paced the length of the bridge. "I've said too much already. Please, Dylan, do not be angry."

"Angry? It's kinda hard not to be. There was a plan to kill me?"

"I am not the only vampire in Florence. I have others I must answer to." He saw the panic across my face. "Please, you must understand what this means."

"Go on, then," I said, trying to stay calm. If he wasn't the only vampire, how many were there? The panic from yesterday was setting in all over again.

"We are typically lone creatures. However, we do have a hierarchy…a government, if you will, to handle certain situations. I was not the only one who heard your thoughts that evening at the bistro. We had a meeting about whether something should be done about you or not. Truth seekers are usually taken out to prevent learning about us. I volunteered to take care of it."

I shuddered involuntarily at how he said the last part. *Take care of it.* I didn't know if I should be completely terrified now or relieved that it was Nico who had volunteered.

"Do they know you let me live?"

He nodded once and seated himself beside me again. "They do. That's why I was running late this evening. They are not happy about it, but they have given me some choices." I noticed he didn't seem happy about it.

I watched the internal battle on his face. I wanted to know what these options were since they obviously concerned me. "And?" I finally asked, hoping they wouldn't be too horrible.

"Oh Dylan, I'm so sorry." There was silence for a long time before he spoke again. "None of this was supposed to happen. It was supposed to be simple, and I let it get out of control."

"I guess I should be thankful for that," I remarked under my breath. He was going to kill me that evening. Thankfully, I had said something to the shop owner in passing or Nico would never have stopped and then….

It was too much to process.

Nico rested his face in his hands and shook his head. "Don't be thankful yet."

"Just tell me." I was hoping it could be like a bandage

– just rip it off and get it out of the way.

"I can either make you my pet or kill you." I felt like there was an echo as what he said reverberated and beat through the sides of my skull.

"Your pet? What does that even *mean?*"

I'm not sure if it even really mattered because obviously whatever a pet was had to be better than death. Right?

He wouldn't make eye contact with me and I knew it was bad. Really bad. "It's what we call someone we groom before turning them. If it's what you choose, you'll be a vampire within the next year, or – they'll see to it that you die."

My eyes felt like they were on fire, the burning was so bad. "I'm – I'm going to be groomed to be a vampire?" I asked, hardly able to say the words out loud. I raised a hand to wipe tears beginning to trickle down my cheek. I didn't know how to get myself out of this one. To dream about immortality was one thing, yet to be forced into it was another. I could only choose vampire because death was not something I was ready for. Though, vampire was not at the top of my "to do" list.

"Then you've decided? That simply?" He asked, sounding surprised which option I had chosen.

I looked at him, bewildered. "Do I really have a

choice? Of course I'd pick that over death."

I couldn't get the idea he was keeping this from me out of my head. There had actually been a meeting about whether I should be allowed to live or not. I had goose bumps across my skin and it had nothing to do with the temperature. "When were you going to tell me about all of this?"

"Tonight." He shrugged. "It was just a matter of privacy."

"It's clear why you've been so honest tonight," I countered, filling in the missing pieces.

Nico nodded slowly. "That's the reason I was willing to answer all of your questions. No one can ever actually know what we are and what we do. As soon as you left Transylvania and didn't return home, you were a target." He moved in closer and wrapped his arms around me and pulled me against his chest. "Tell me I did the right thing, Dylan. Tell me saving you was the right thing."

His breath was cool on my ear.

I knew he had to have felt as torn as I was. Killing me that night would have been a lot easier than putting me through this. Now things were complicated and he had people watching what he was doing. I imagine it was probably better to fly under the radar with this hierarchy he had spoken of. He had risked his place with the other vampires to save me. But there were consequences for his actions and I would be the one to face them.

He watched me intently and waited for me to say something and let him know that he *had* done the right thing. I felt like I was going to hyperventilate. I had known him less than twenty four hours and yet no matter what he did around me, I ended up breathless.

"Oh, *mia mortale*...I'm so sorry," he whispered as he kissed the top of my head.

"No, I mean...I didn't *want* to die in the alley. Of course I didn't. I don't know what I was thinking looking for vampires. I was bored with my life. And now," I choked on a sob. "And now?"

Chapter 5

SEVERAL DAYS HAD passed before I saw Nico again. I had asked for some alone time to soak in everything that had just transpired and he had given it to me, too. Maybe it was even a little too much time.

I had spent the first night crying myself to sleep with uncontrollable sobbing that forced me to get a new pillowcase out of the closet.

On the second night, I thought of every different possibility to get me out of this situation. I could go to the police. The idea ended quickly when I remembered the other vampires and the whole mind reading thing. They'd kill me before I even made it to the station. I could run screaming back to Florida. It sounded like a bad idea, though. First, I wouldn't give my friends the satisfaction. Also, I didn't want to run.

The third night I wrote a list of pros and cons of being alive. I didn't get very far, which didn't help matters. As depression set in, I got hungry and called room service. I ordered almost everything on the menu. I spent the rest of the night sick to my stomach and shredding my list. Leaving Florida was something I was glad I did. Saying goodbye to my friends was hard, but I'd get over that, too, in time. Leaving mortality behind? It was something a little more difficult to swallow. I knew there was a danger to seeking the truth when I departed for this trip, but nothing ever happened to the other truth seekers, so why me? The reasonable part of me felt certain that I wouldn't find a vampire. It was just something to do. I was sure that vampires didn't exist, but they do and I still can't believe it.

This whole time, I hardly stepped out of the hotel room. I was scared of too many things. Of seeing Nico and not seeing him and the idea of running into another vampire who maybe *would* have killed me in the alley. How many times had I passed by one of them during my walks in the city and not known it? I would have to ask Nico about that, though I wasn't sure if I wanted to know the answer.

I left the room three times in total.

The first was to talk to Matt down at Yankee Bar, which I made sure to visit in the brightest part of the day.

The position was mine if I wanted it. I was scheduled to start next Tuesday and would be paid in cash tips, so we didn't have to worry about reporting anything. I had told him that it was only temporary because I needed some extra cash to extend my vacation. He understood; apparently, he's used to it.

The second place I went was the little grocery store around the corner to get some groceries. I wanted to make sure there was enough to eat while holed up in the little hotel room. Thank goodness for my mini fridge and the little microwave.

Finally, I left the room one last time to talk to the hotel manager down in the lobby. It was time to negotiate some sort of weekly rate. He wanted to know how long I'd be staying but I didn't have an answer. I told him it was yet to be determined but it was easier to figure out in weeks instead of days anymore. He cut me a good deal and I was thankful because it saved me over a hundred Euros a week.

It was Saturday by the time I finally met up with Nico and I was willing to go along with whatever he had in mind. The idea of becoming immortal had its benefits, though whether I was thinking sane or not was undetermined. It was better than anything waiting for me back in Florida. It's not like I had some plan of what I was going to do once I was done traipsing across Europe. My bank account was beyond depleted and I knew it was time to head back. Hopefully the bartending was going to help soften the blow to my finances. I wasn't ready to let it all end and go back to stress and suffering. Immortality had its upsides. I was always complaining that I didn't have enough time to do things I wanted to. It's funny how things work out.

Nico also awakened feelings inside of me I thought had died with my wedding bouquet. As much as I hated being forced into immortality, I couldn't get the feel of his lips on my skin out of my head. I just wished we had actually kissed again before he told me about the plan. I didn't want him to change his mind about what we both wanted to happen, or at least I *think* he wanted the same thing. No matter how delusional I was, a vampire boyfriend isn't exactly what I was expecting when I arrived in Italy. I'm not even sure how it works, but I'm too involved to turn back now. What was so great about being a plain old mortal anyways? I had a year to decide.

***

"So, a year?" I asked as we strolled along. It was just after one in the morning when we sat down on the stairs inside Boboli Gardens. "What goes on during this year?"

The statue of Neptune stood before us, spewing

water into the pond. Nico positioned me so I sat on a step just below him with his legs on either side of me. His arms wrapped around the tops of my shoulders. Despite the temperature dropping outside, I found myself getting warmer as his fingertips danced across my shoulders. "Well, I explain to you the history which will become yours. You will watch me hunt so you know what it is that you will become."

"I will watch you hunt?" The visual that popped into my head left me aghast.

"Yes. You'll need to know what to do so you can feed your thirst. And so there are no surprises."

"What else?"

"Well, we will meet some of the other vampires around so you can ask questions of them, as well."

It didn't sound too exciting. Actually, I wasn't looking forward to meeting any other vampires. I had a feeling Nico was different than them and I didn't want to find out exactly what those differences were until I was on a level playing field with them and had some sort of self-defense.

"And?" I questioned, turning to watch his facial expressions.

He smiled. "You want more? Well, there's the vampire law and you learn about the hierarchy I spoke of before. We are free to move about, but there are rules to be followed at all times."

"And?" I grinned, enjoying the game. These were good things to know, but I wanted something more interesting to focus on.

"And, we enjoy each other's company," he sighed as he tightened his hold around me.

And make love over and over and over, I added silently. As soon as I let the thought float into my head, I regretted it, feeling my cheeks burning with a furious flush, knowing he was reading my thoughts.

"Yes, we could do that, too." Nico moved so quickly that he was on the same step as I was before I could blink. His fingers held my chin ever so delicately and his eyes stared into mine, as if asking for permission.

I licked my lips unconsciously, which he took as the sign he needed for our first consensual kiss. His lips hesitated over mine for several seconds. I reached up slowly and took the back of his neck with both of my hands as my fingers danced along his hairline. He met the gap and our lips melted together. His tongue traced my lip and I opened my mouth, inviting him deeper. The intensity strengthened as he accepted and continued the kiss. My heart felt like it was going to beat right out of my chest and I pulled back, gasping for air.

"Wow," I managed while backing up to another step to balance myself. My whole body was trembling uncontrollably.

Nico moved up the same step to stay close to me. He leaned in for another kiss, seeming to be equally pulled to me as I was to him. I just didn't know if my body could handle it. When he was touching me, I felt like every cell in my body was going to burst.

"We need some privacy," I said quietly, looking around, becoming very aware that we were completely exposed to any curious visitors of the gardens.

"Not tonight, I'm afraid," he frowned, looking up at the night sky.

"Why?" My eagerness surprised me. I was offering myself to him without hesitation.

"The sun will be coming up before I can get you somewhere private and…." He trailed off.

I nodded. It was beginning to make sense. "Soon, perhaps?"

He smiled at my voracity. "Yes, perhaps soon. Until then, let me at least take you back to your hotel."

I nodded. "You know, I'm supposed to fly back to Florida tomorrow. My three weeks are up." I had seen the plane ticket on my desk earlier today and had spent entirely too much time staring at it, trying to figure out what it all meant.

Nico looked at me with a sullen expression. "You

know you can't, right?"

"I know. I don't know what I'm supposed to do, though. My best friend has my itinerary. She's going to expect me back." Not getting on that plane to go home wouldn't be something easy for me. Had I known I wasn't ever going to see her or any of my other friends again, I would have spent longer saying goodbye or something.

"You've made this choice. It won't be easy right away, but after a while, she and everyone you know will have passed."

Wow, how morbid. I knew he was right, but this might actually be harder than I expected. "What about some sort of contact?"

"How do you mean? Calling them?" He shook his head and avoided making eye contact with me. I saw him frown and knew it was hard for him to tell me. "Think about it – what could you possibly say?" He squeezed my shoulder to try offering me some sort of comfort. I looked away from him and stood up from the step. I went down a few stairs and ran my hand along the railing. In the distance, the city lights twinkled, just beyond the trees and the outline of Palazzo Pitti.

I knew he was right, but I didn't want to leave my friends hanging, either. I had roots in Florida and not returning would be strange. Like Nico said, maybe it wouldn't bother me after a few decades, once everyone I knew was gone.

I stood awkwardly, realizing my feet were sore from walking around the city. Maybe he didn't get tired, but I was only human, after all.

Something else hit me. "What about my clothes? My things?"

He scratched the bridge of his nose. "What?"

"All of my belongings. I only have a limited amount of clothes here. All my belongings…my entire life…it's all in Florida." My mind swam with the contents of my apartment, my books, my collection of shoes, my everything. Leaving that for someone to dig through was unacceptable.

Nico sighed and took a few steps in front of me. His slim physique was a dark shadow in front of me as he peered in the direction of the Duomo, its rounded rooftop peaking up over the trees.

"Nico?" I asked again.

He turned to face me and stared at my boots instead of my face. I shifted and realized that he was avoiding answering my concern.

My head dropped and I sat down on the bench in front of me. "It's gone, isn't it? I have to rebuild everything here."

Nico glanced up at me and took a step forward. "Yes.

I feel like I keep apologizing to you since I've met you, but again, I'm sorry."

I stood up again and grimaced, my boots digging into my ankles.

"What's the matter?" He asked, seeing the hint of pain shoot across my face.

"I could say *everything*. But to start with, these boots are killing me."

Nico scooped me off my feet. "Allow me." Before I could ask what he was doing, he bounded up the stairs and jumped onto the roof. I fought the urge to scream because I knew it wouldn't be a good idea. He sensed my nervousness and brushed my lips with his own. We were suddenly flying across the rooftops of Florence.

He set me down around the corner from the hotel and it was hard for me to catch my breath. He, on the other hand, hadn't even broken a sweat.

"That only solves one problem," I said dryly. "My life? My clothes? My everything?"

"Dylan, I don't know what to say. We can rebuild together, but you cannot go back. Not only would it be too dangerous, it could never be allowed. In time, you will overcome the issue.

"Hmmmph." I knew he was right, but I could still be pissed off about it for a little while longer.

He took my hand and we walked down the sidewalk. We turned the corner like any normal couple, holding hands and staying in stride. He lowered his head and his lips brushed mine in a farewell kiss. Then he was gone before I could ask him when I'd see him again.

Chapter 6

I DRESSED IN black pants and a turquoise sequined top and comfortable black shoes. I'd dipped into my credit card yet again for some more shopping because boots weren't an option. There was no point avoiding debt now since the credit card companies wouldn't be able to find me. They could clear out my apartment and take my car, too. There was no way to go back for it, anyway.

It was my first night bartending at Yankee Bar and I wanted to make sure my feet were up to it. Inside, the bar looked modest enough with wood paneled walls and frosted glass chandeliers hanging low to add ambience. A simple hostess stand was in front with a menu under a pane of glass. Tables were staggered throughout the room with red linens across them and blue napkins, obviously capitalizing on the

American aspect of the place.

Matt greeted me and showed me over to the bar. "We have just about every kind of alcohol you can imagine." He showed me the back wall where all the bottles were done alphabetically rather than by type. This might get confusing, but I started to read all the labels, getting a sense for what was available.

"What are some of the favorites?" I asked, picking up a bottle of Strega and giving it a smell. It smelled a lot like Galliano, but a little stronger on the fennel.

"The Bellini, but a lot of people will ask what your favorite drink is, so be creative."

I looked around the sink for the different fruits and then bent down to the small fridge. I glanced up at him. "Do you have Red Bull?"

He gave me a strange look. "Yes, in the back. We don't really sell much of it. What did you have in mind?"

"It's not a big seller? Really? Then you haven't had the right bartender here. Red Bull in drinks is huge back in the States right now. You'll want to get some more in. I promise you that we're going to go through a ton while I'm here."

He laughed at my enthusiasm and made a note of it. "Okay, you got it. Anything else we need?"

I peered around some more. It appeared as though I

had everything else, including flavored vodkas, cherries, bottle opener, and a blender. "Lighter?"

"There's no smoking in Italy. They banned it a few years back."

I shook my head. "It's for lighting drinks on fire, not cigarettes."

"Oh, right. We haven't gotten into that here. You think people will order them?"

I shrugged. "It's worth a try. Back home, once you lit one on fire, everyone else wanted one, too."

"I'll get one for you before the rush gets here. Looks like you've got things under control for now. Get yourself comfortable." He looked at his watch. "It's five now. The rush starts at six and then we'll be balls to the wall until we close at twelve."

Midnight. It was one of the reasons I took this job. It kept me up later and I still got off in plenty of time to see plenty of Nico.

I placed a couple beer steins in the reach-in freezer to get cold for the rush and finished stocking the fruit purees along the side of the cooler. Another bartender slid in next to me. His black hair greased straight back and his bronzed skin showing off his lack of chest hairs as his button down shirt was missing the top four buttons or so.

He extended his hand. "Giancarlo. You must be

Dylan. Matt's been talking about you and some of the new drinks you're going to show us how to make."

I shook his hand and was shocked with the warmth in it. "Oh yeah? I look forward to it. Nice to meet you." His accent was thick but still spoke better English than I expected.

Matt passed by. "I see you two have met."

I nodded.

He tossed me a lighter. "Have fun."

Giancarlo reached into the bottles in the well and pulled out a bottle of Sambuca. He grabbed two shot glasses and filled each to the rim. One was slid in my direction and he made a gesture with his hand.

I gave it a sniff. Very strong anise, which meant I wasn't going to like it. I don't like any of those, but then again I didn't like black licorice, either. I shook my head.

"Suit yourself," he said, quickly downing the shot and then reaching for mine, he asked me for my lighter. I reached over and handed it to him. "Matt says you're into drinks that light up."

I agreed. "Yes, but...Sambuca?"

"Just watch," he said, grabbing an empty glass beside it. "This is called a flaming Sambuca. I had those years ago, but I never made them at the bar. Our usual bartenders can't usually handle this sort of thing, so just remember you started it."

He held the lighter above the glass and the Sambuca caught on fire with a bright blue flame. He quickly poured the flaming liquid into the other glass, then placed the first glass upside down over the liquid. He carried the two glasses on top of each other to directly in front of me, moving the top glass to sit upside down on the bar.

"Now do the shot," he said handing me the glass. I noticed Matt standing in the corner and watching both of us. I looked at him quickly for approval and after I saw him nod, I downed the shot. Giancarlo handed me a straw. "Now put the straw under this glass and suck the fumes."

Whoa. This was something totally different. "Do what?" I asked, holding the straw awkwardly.

He quickly demonstrated and I did as told. I held the straw just under the glass as he showed me. I came up coughing and feeling like I just did something illegal. "The kids will love it, trust me."

A few guys at the end of the bar gave a chuckle and I quickly shot them a look.

At one point during the night, there were two rows of people waiting to get drinks. Money was waving in all directions to get everything from a bottle of beer to a special concoction of my or Giancarlo's desires. I poured shots of various liquors and shook martini shakers all night long. My shoulders were sore from reaching for bottles off the bar all night, but as I watched the tip jar fill up, the pain dulled and eventually faded altogether.

We stayed busy all the way until we closed the doors, just as Matt had promised. Closing the doors was quite literal tonight as we had to force the last of the drinkers off their bar stools and out the door. It was refreshing from my days as a restaurant manager where stragglers could stay and hold up our closing for hours. Here, closing time meant leaving time. I liked it. I reveled in the freedom of bartending and forgot how much I enjoyed working and being in the moment. I had gotten stuck in management back home and hated the stress. At the bar tonight, it was just fun, especially when I got the hang of serving flaming Sambucas and teaching Giancarlo how to do a few drinks that were popular in the States.

I walked out of the back door of the bar with a promise to be back in a few days for my next shift. I found comfort with the wad of cash I had in my pocket. Extra cash was an understatement, I thought to myself, having counted over a hundred euros from my share of the tip jar. A couple nights a week at this rate and I could get my wardrobe back up to standards in no time.

I cringed, remembering my closet back home.

***

The next morning, after sleeping in entirely too late, I dressed and headed to Via Tornabuoni. I knew I should be saving some of the money towards paying the hotel bill and getting food, but I couldn't resist a little shopping spree. Even if I could only afford a few new tops, it was worth it.

As I entered in my jeans and cotton t-shirt, I was having a Pretty Woman moment where the store clerks sort of stared at me, wondering what brought me in here dressed as I was in their stores. Suddenly I wish they were all too busy arguing with boyfriends on their cell phones to pay any attention to me.

I gave them a slight smile and quickly headed towards the discount racks in the back. After a few minutes, a tall, very thin woman in a tight black dress and strappy heels came up to me and asked if she could help. Her English was better than my Italian was, so I felt comfortable talking with her. I showed her some of the tops I had on my arm, which, while discounted, were still very expensive. She escorted me to the dressing room where I checked the price tags a little more closely and did the math. Yikes! The tops were cute, but at these prices, I could only buy one, so the major decision was the black button down or the red one with silver straps.

After careful deliberation, I brought the red one to

the counter and paid for my purchase. The clerk was unable to hide her shock quickly enough for me not to see when I paid in cash, but she was nice enough. She also told me about a few stores in North Centro, which were a little more affordable. I thanked her profusely for the tip and took a walk up to the area.

Several hours and a large shopping bag later, I was happily walking back into the hotel to unpack my purchases. I had grabbed lunch on the way and was looking forward to an evening of hanging out. There was no work today and getting a distraction from the events of the last few days was much needed.

Chapter 7

A KNOCK AT my hotel room door startled me awake. I had fallen asleep without realizing the time. I had time off from work and last night had exhausted me more than I had realized. I wiped my eyes and looked at the alarm clock next to the bed. It was eleven.

It couldn't be the maid and I was pretty sure that I didn't order room service. I opened the door to find Nico dressed in a red button down and black pants that made him look absolutely delicious. The colors accentuated his pale skin, but rather than looking suspiciously pale, it made him look warmer and more alive. I suddenly cursed myself for not looking at myself in the mirror before opening the door or for shaving my legs in the shower earlier. Dressed in plaid boxers and a tight-fitting green tank top, I was a strong contrast from him.

I should have set an alarm or at least slept in something a little sexier. I pushed my fingers through my hair in an effort to smooth out my bed-head and hoped that he wouldn't notice. I was tempted to tell him to come back in fifteen minutes and close the door, but I kept it open and faced him while still groggy.

"Can I come in?"

His question made me realize the door was still only cracked open. "Of course."

Curiosity was getting the better of me on this one. "Do you *have* to be invited in before you can enter?"

"You never stop, do you?" He grinned, shaking his head. "No, I don't have to be, but it's nice. Another old wives' tale to make people feel safer."

Safe. That's such an odd term now I think of it. *I'm dating a vampire…yeah, that's safe.*

Nico closed the door and the distance between us. "I'm not going to hurt you. You know this, right?"

"Y-yes," I whispered. I prayed like hell I was right on this, but I was too far gone. There was no way I was going to push Nico away.

"Not on purpose, anyways," he said smiling, his fangs just slightly visible. "Cute outfit. It's not what I expected."

I let out a soft sigh. I was nervous but in a strange,

butterfly-in-the-stomach sort of way. It was hard to explain. He walked through the small room and took his time on everything. He trailed a finger across the cluttered desk mindlessly and ventured, "So, what are you doing tonight?"

"Umm, hadn't really thought about it yet." I hadn't wanted to tell him anything past that or admit I fell asleep and was planning on staying asleep. "I'll be right back," I said, slipping around the corner.

I took this time to disappear into the bathroom. If I could just get a brush through my hair and find the mouthwash somewhere in here. I dumped out my makeup case in the sink, hurrying. In an attempt at speed, half my mouthwash fell down the drain, narrowly missing my hair brush. I didn't have time for a lot of makeup, so I went for the basics. I tried for small talk to stall while I did as much as I could. "So I got a job."

"What?" He asked from the other room. "Why did you do that?"

I laughed and continued to brush out the knots in my hair. "I'm out of money and need to continue to pay for this hotel for a while. There is an American bar not far from here that was looking for a bartender. Italian isn't required but English is a must."

I heard the bed squeak and knew he was sitting on it. I resisted the urge to look and continued to make quick work of a presentable version of myself. "What do you think?"

"I think this bed is very comfortable," he called from the next room.

Shit. I let the hairbrush fall into the sink and hesitated, almost scared to leave the bathroom.

"*Vieni qui*," he called to me, amusement in his voice.

I left my hand on the door frame.

He smiled, dimples just reaching his cheeks. "It means come here."

A breath left my lips. "I know what it means."

As if drawn to the sound of his voice alone, I walked to the edge of the bed. His Italian could get me to walk to the ends of the Earth. I wasn't sure if it was just him or if it was a vampire thing. My eyes were glued to him. I didn't care what the answer was. I watched as he slowly unbuttoned his shirt to expose an inch of pale, muscled skin with each released button. My throat was growing dry with anticipation. My feet were attempting to stay planted on the ground, fighting the urge to push him onto the bed and ravage him.

"Dylan," Nico spoke. "Come closer."

I took a step towards him.

"Closer," he repeated.

I took another step forward, as though in a trance. Each time he spoke, something took a hold of me and moved me closer to him until I was within arm's reach of him. I opened my mouth to speak but didn't trust my vocal cords to actually work.

His arms reached out and encircled my waist. He pulled me to him so I was standing between his legs where he sat, naked from the waist up. I looked slowly from his belt to the small dark curve of hairs traveling to just above his naval. From there, it was completely smooth the rest of the way up his chiseled chest. I knew I was staring, but had to make sure the mental image was well catalogued for a long time. He pulled me onto his lap so my legs were straddling him.

We sat there, eyes locked for several moments before he spoke. "Tell me what you want." His frigid fingers played with the spaghetti strap of my tank top, sliding it up and down my shoulder. He knew what I wanted but he was going to make me say it.

"You." I couldn't believe this was actually happening. I listened for any sounds out in the hall, but heard nothing. I didn't want any interruptions.

In a single movement, I was laying on the bed and he was on top of me and sliding a hand under me to guide my tank top off. There was no bra since the tank had one built in. He seemed shocked by this realization and cupped my breasts with his strong hands.

"Dylan, these are beautiful." He kissed the top of each one.

I glanced away, feeling apprehensive about what was about to happen.

When I looked up, I found his sapphire blue eyes piercing into me.

"You don't believe me?"

I shrugged, not wanting to admit the insecurities I had about my body.

"Look at me."

I stared up into his face. This was something I wanted more than anything I could think of, which terrified and exhilarated me at the same time. Chris was the last man I had slept with and that was months ago. The sexual tension had been building in me for a while now and the release was desperately needed.

His mouth settled onto mine and I returned his kisses with as much fervor as he gave. I ran my tongue along his lips and let them trail to his fangs. I hesitated a little, and the exploration continued further. My hands ran lower, playing on his belt buckle.

Startled by my eagerness, his mouth moved too fast from mine. I tasted the wound immediately and froze, unsure of how to proceed. The coppery taste of blood stung in my mouth where his fang nicked my lip. My tongue moved outwards on my lip to assess the damage.

Nico inched towards me, watching my eyes for any

sign of my thoughts. The room seemed to move in slow motion as he reached forward, holding my chin in the palm of his hand.

"Let me," he begged as he moved his lips closer to my face.

I stayed frozen in place in an attempt to decide if this was a good idea or not. Before I had a chance to object, his lips were on the injured area and his tongue slid gently along the wound. He gently sucked on my bottom lip while he stared into my eyes, assuring me it was okay. I closed my eyes and let myself relax again as he continued to probe my mouth with his tongue and remove all evidence of the accident.

"All better," he finally said while pulling back.

My finger touched my lip. "It's gone?" I already knew the answer, but it still came out like a question.

He smiled at my naivety. "Yes, mia mortale, it's gone." He kissed me softly on the lips. "I didn't mean for that to happen. You just surprised me."

"I-it's okay," I laid back down on the bed with my head hitting the pillow. More questions were spinning through my mind but they disappeared when I looked up at Nico.

As I watched his approach, I smiled up at him. His hands effortlessly removed his belt and as his pants slid down the length of his legs. I kept wondering about *how* this was going to happen. Technically Nico was dead—or undead, but still. There was no blood flow, so how was he going to perform?

His briefs stood away from his body eagerly and while I knew he'd have no problem with what was inevitably going to occur, the question of how was still at the tip of my tongue.

He must have seen my expression because he paused suddenly. "Yes?"

"Hmmm?" I asked, not wanting to let on what I was thinking about. My panties were already flooding with my own anticipation.

"You have more questions, so go ahead," he said patiently while leaning his elbow against my pillow. He played with the edge of my boxers and gently tugged at them.

"No, nothing." This was too embarrassing of a thought to share out loud.

"Dylan, just ask...."

I bit the corner of my lip, mortified that I was actually going to repeat my question aloud. "Well, how do you get enough blood flow to, well...." I angled my glance down at him, hoping he wouldn't make me say the rest.

Laughter filled the room. "Dylan, Dylan, we're about to make love and *that's* what's going through your head?"

I felt the burning sensation rise up my cheeks. "I

know, I know -."

"It just requires a little blood. I fed before coming over here so things could work. Without feeding, then -," he paused, "we wouldn't be able to do this." His hands wandered up my chest and traced the side of my breasts.

"Oh." My mind was spinning. Someone died earlier just so I could have sex, It didn't seem right. Was I just as much of a monster as he was for allowing it? Granted, I didn't know that's what it took, even though I had read enough vampire erotica to know how it was supposed to work.

"Dylan?"

I looked at him but felt like my humanity was slipping away.

"I didn't kill anyone," he assured. "I just had a little drink."

What? Now I was completely confused. How can he possibly just take a little drink off of someone without them noticing? I certainly would have noticed, not to mention the fang marks to give it away....

Nico let out a sigh before he sat up in bed, ready to give a full explanation. He reached out, pulling me into his lap. "This is all going to make a lot more sense in a year, but I'll try my best."

I desperately wanted to pull him back down to the

bed and tell him to forget it, yet curiosity was getting the best of me. My nipples ached to be kissed again and I let the hardness of his body embrace me.

"I can wash away recent memories. There was a man earlier that was in the wrong place at the wrong time. He stepped in front of me, I pulled him into a quick hold, took a few, umm, sips, if you will. It was no more than half a pint – less than what you'd donate at a blood bank. There's a bit of mind control which goes with it, but there's no danger. I take what I need, and then, well, remember what happened to your lip?"

"Yes," I said, my finger automatically tracing my bottom lip.

"Our saliva has a sort of healing mechanism in it. Once applied, any marks heal almost instantly, so there will never be bite marks for this man to see later. Then I wash away the memory of me being there and he walks away thinking he had one too many beers at the pub. These little sips aren't enough to last a few days, but it helps spread out the full feedings over a week or so. The sips help to give me enough blood for—well, you already know that."

"Which is why your face can flush at certain times, too?" I asked, calling him out on the redness filling out in his cheeks.

He chuckled softly, "Yes."

"Well," I said, growing bolder I leaned back against the bed, "*Vieni qui.*"

"Whatever you want," he moaned, leaning across my body and closing the gap between our lips again.

Cold fingertips played along my back and his mouth kissed my shoulders. The touch of his skin sent my nipples into a hardened state instantly. He kneaded them in his fingertips and his eyes never left mine.

I draped my arms about his neck and let my fingertips play in the curly hairs at the bottom of his hairline.

His skilled hands traveled down the length of my body and came to rest along my side. My hips rose to meet him so I did not lose too much contact with him.

He broke the kiss. "Slow down. I want to take my time with you. This is all about you. We can go all night if you like…."

Nico was already going to have to peel me out of my panties. Waiting or going slow wasn't something I could handle but I nodded anyway in hopes of changing his mind somewhere along the way. And all night? He might have enough stamina for all night but I've been out of practice. I doubted my own abilities. I was only mortal, after all.

His mouth moved along my jaw, down the length of my neck. As the blood beat faster through my veins at the base of my throat, my breath caught. Fangs trailed down my skin and left goose bumps along every inch of exposed flesh.

"Mmmm," he moaned against my skin. The cold breath heated things up another degree. My one hand left his neck to trail down lower to his hips. Just as I was able to loop a fingertip into the edge of his briefs, he stopped and closed his hand around my own. "Not yet."

My hand stopped in mid-motion but didn't retreat.

"Back around my neck," he said with a grin. "Keep them there."

I desperately wanted to get my fingers around the part of Nico that was anxiously pressed against my thigh.

My fingers released his briefs and they trailed ever so slowly up the length of his chest, my nails dragging across his nipples as soft sighs escaped his lips. As my hand finally made its way up to his neck again, he let his own fingers explore.

His hands left my hips and traveled lower still until they were on my inner thighs. Cold fingertips brushed my boxers aside and his fingers were creeping under the elastic of my panties.

My breath caught and my hands clenched tighter around his neck in anticipation of what would come next. "Nico." I didn't want him to stop.

I was already soaked, but that was nothing. He slid his fingers past the elastic and his middle one entered me ever so slowly. A growl escaped his lips and his finger pushed deeper.

"Dylan," he sounded surprised. Maybe now that he realized how wet I was, he'd realize why I didn't want him to slow down.

My hips rose off the bed slightly, sending his finger still deeper. His other hand left my inner thigh and pushed me gently back onto the bed.

Suddenly the panties were too restricting. I wanted more. And fast. A second finger entered me and they worked me over like he was typing on a keyboard. My breathing sped up and his mouth covered mine, eating my gasps as though they were dinner.

I squirmed a little more, hoping to get these panties off.

"Everything okay?" he asked, his fingers stopping and sliding out unconsciously.

My hips rose up again. "Off, take them off," I said. My raspy voice pushed beyond the pulse in my throat.

His hands obeyed and grabbed the thin material at both sides. He pulled them down my legs and flung them somewhere in the room. I didn't care where.

Without missing a beat, his fingers were back to where they had been as if there hadn't been an interruption. His eyes soaked into mine and I laid beneath him, completely bare, willing for him to take me at any moment.

With my hands still around his neck, I used them to

pull his mouth onto mine again. As he leaned in to my demand, I arched myself up the length of his body. I felt as eager as he did for things to continue.

I released the hold around his neck and my fingers wrapped around his eagerness before he had a chance to protest. The hunger in his eyes told me he wasn't going to tell me to slow down this time. Every inch of him was rock hard and surprisingly hot, compared to the rest of his body…unless it was just my body that was on fire.

Nudging at him, I guided his briefs down his legs. He pulled away for just a moment, sending his undergarments flying in the same general direction as my panties had gone only minutes before.

He perched himself above me, staring at me with a desire that equaled mine. I peered down the length of our bodies to where he was about to enter. I shifted slightly, trying to get him in without seeming too eager.

"Once we start, mia mortale, I will not be able to stop," he warned. "I have not taken a lover to my bed in over a century."

The words spun in my head. Lover. Bed. Not the point he was trying to make, but there it was. I nodded and then he gave me exactly what I wanted.

He was gentle – at first. The want turned into need quicker than either of us had anticipated. Each of his thrusts sent me screaming over the edge and he ended up handing me a pillow to scream into so as not to alert the hotel staff. He was so much stronger than anyone else I'd ever been with – for obvious reasons. Then there was his size. I wasn't a virgin but with him, I may as well have been. After my voice was raspy from screaming joyously, we finally found a rhythm suiting us both which seemed to go on for hours.

His mouth floated from my shoulders, to the base of my throat, to my lips, and back again. His fingers slid from my swollen nipples to my abdomen, to all the lower places making me scream out all over again. The coldness of his fingers acted as a catalyst against my feverish skin, causing both of us to crave each other's flesh even more than we thought possible. He moved his hands to brace my shoulders as his body came to climax. I made a small sound of discomfort as the strength of him dug through my body. The pain quickly turned to waves of pleasure crashing over my body rapidly and unexpectedly.

He was blindly grabbing a wad of the comforter, pulsating forward, harder than before. I let out one last muffled scream as we collapsed into a pile on the bed. A sound of contentment escaped from his lips. Sweat was dripping from every pore of my body and I lay gasping for air, with a grin across my face.

He lay next to me, smiling. "Thank you."

My breath was finally returning in short puffs, which I was struggling to hide. "No, thank you," I managed.

"Are you okay?"

"Mmm hmm."

I stretched out across the bed, satisfied. When I stretched, there was suddenly a shooting pain down the length of my body. I winced.

"Did I hurt you?" He asked, concern deep in his voice.

Uh oh. I tried to ignore him. Maybe if I just laid here for a few more minutes, the pain would go away.

"I did, didn't I?"

Before I could argue, he was inspecting me, looking for bruises. I had no doubt that there would be some, though it would take a few days for them to surface.

He seemed horrified that he had hurt me, though he didn't say anything. His expression said it all.

"It was worth it," I assured him, kissing him gently.

Chapter 8

NICO LACED MY fingers with his as we walked across the Ponte Santa Trinita. "Want to go for drinks? There are still a few places open."

I nodded. There was no way I was ready to sleep after what I had just experienced. We went up to a trendy little bar called Dolce Vita. The place was nothing to look at from the sidewalk. In amongst a video store and a gelateria, it would be easy to pass it during the day without ever knowing it was there. Tonight, however, it was crowded and a line of people stood out front to get in. Crowds were good because he wouldn't attract any undue attention. He was a gorgeous creature, so women were always eyeing him, though tonight his eyes were only on me.

I started to go towards the end of the line when he

grabbed my elbow.

"Where are you going?" He asked, amusement showing across his face.

I nodded towards the back.

He chuckled. "Come with me."

We made our way up to the front and past all the people who appeared a little annoyed that we were jumping in front. Nico led us right in the front door and gave a nod to the security guard.

"Nice," I commented. He just smiled and led me further into the club.

Strobe lights flashed through the bar and made it difficult to get my bearings. Women were literally throwing themselves in our path and he simply flashed his award-winning smile at them and pushed past, holding my hand. The bartenders nodded in his direction. We squeezed past a crowd and to the wine bar in a separate room with no strobes or dancing so I could get a glass of wine.

"Sangria," I said over the noise to the bartender.

Nico placed his hand over mine and shook his head. "Chianti," he corrected.

The bartender set a glass in front of me and I picked it up with a frown.

"Why Chianti?"

"Why not?" Nico challenged. "You're in Italy, not

Spain."

"Hmmph," I said, taking a sip and following him into the next room.

The back room glowed with a soft blue-green light. We were able to get a plush couch in the corner to sit in, which is prime real estate in a place like this.

The club was smaller than it looked from the outside. It was essentially two small rooms with ample seating and two bars, along with seating outside that nobody chose unless they had no other options. Luckily, that was not the case for us.

I sunk into the purple leather and watched as people mingled with one another, going in and out of the two rooms as music and smoke filled the place. Black paint covered the walls and a single window across the room from me showed there was still plenty of night left and a line of people waiting to get in to enjoy themselves.

I looked over at Nico and watched another woman play coy with him as she crossed the room.

"What?" He asked innocently.

I raised my eyebrows. "Everyone seems very friendly." I clung close to him to make sure everyone in the club knew I was with him and so he could hear me over the volume of the music.

The corners of his mouth quivered. "Perhaps. Are

you hinting at something?"

There was something he wasn't admitting to. "Why do the bartenders seem to know you?"

"Do they?"

"Yes."

"I hadn't noticed."

"The women seem very friendly, too," I added, unable to hide the jealousy sneaking out. So much for avoiding undue attention.

"I may have come here before." He peered around as if trying to locate someone he knew but quickly turned his attention back to me.

"Oh?"

"A sip or two – or three," he laughed softly.

"Really?"

"It is nothing, truly," he whispered in my ear, taking my hand. "It is simply so busy here that no one notices."

"Hmmm," I commented, sipping my wine.

"Do you like it?"

"What?"

"The wine," Nico said, pointing at my glass.

I wrinkled my nose. "It's oakier than I like."

"You mean it's not fruity."

"I didn't say that, but since you did, yes."

"Wine isn't meant to be fruity."

"Says you," I commented, taking another sip.

He shook his head. "No, says all Italians."

"I could probably get used to it," I admitted.

"I've secured you an apartment near my domicile," Nico announced, holding my hand open and dangling a set of keys above it. He said it so nonchalantly I thought I misheard him.

I let the keys drop into the palm of my hand. "An apartment?"

"You can't keep living out of suitcases and paying by the night here – you've got to be running out of money, which is why I suppose you took a job. And since you'll need a place for the next year...."

He had no idea how much money I was out of. "Okay, so where is this place?" I asked, willing to go along with anything at this point. An apartment in Florence...I could get used to this lifestyle.

"It's in San Marco, clear across the city from where you're staying now. It's a second floor apartment of a palazzo just outside of the Piazza di Duomo."

"And it's how far from where you live?" I asked, hoping he'd finally tell me.

He smiled in his usual charming manner. "Nearby."

"And how much is this apartment I'm staying at?"

"Don't worry about it," he said, watching me intently

as I drank my wine quicker than I should be. "I've got it covered. You don't have to keep bartending if you don't want to."

"I'm enjoying it, so I'll keep it up for a while. Besides, I have expensive taste in clothes, so now I can buy more." I grinned and felt a wave of questions coming on, but knew not to ask all of them at once, so I settled for the basics. "Can you afford it?"

He laughed. "You have so much to learn about me, but not yet. Yes, I can afford it. I told you not to worry about it."

"Okay, okay." I chewed on my bottom lip unconsciously as I looked over at him, trying to read his thoughts.

"Don't worry so much. I own the building you'll be staying in. As for the rest, I've got it covered." He kissed my cheek, took the empty glass out of my hand, and froze.

I felt his whole body language change and his wide shoulders stiffened. He stood up from the couch abruptly, brushed his hand through his hair and cocked his head slightly. He appeared to be listening to something I couldn't hear.

"Everything okay?" I asked, looking up at him.

He raised my empty glass up, but wasn't really looking at me. "Did you want another?"

"Sure." I leaned forward to see where he disappeared to but it was as though he vanished into thin air. Settling back on the couch, I listened to the music, which was much different from anything they were playing back in the States. It had a Brazilian feel to it with a strong bass that seemed to pound through my whole body. I watched the strobes flash through the next room where people were practically standing on top of each other to dance. It was such a shame people were packed in here like sardines with all the art on the walls from different local artists. Each to their own, I guess.

I felt the cushion give a little beside me.

"That was quick," I said, turning just in time to realize it wasn't Nico. "Oh, I'm sorry, I thought you were someone else."

"No, no I'm not. But I'm glad that I caught you without him for a minute." The man's voice carried an accent heavily Italian. He watched me through bluish-grey eyes and impossibly long eyelashes. His pitch black hair was pulled into a tight ponytail hanging just at shoulder length.

I was startled by his forwardness. "I'm really not interested," I said as I stood to search for Nico. The bar area was packed and I couldn't spot him out of the crowd.

"I didn't ask you if you were," the dark-haired stranger replied.

I took a step away from him, hoping Nico could hear this conversation and come rescue me – sooner than later.

"Why don't you sit back down," the man suggested, pointing to the empty spot next to him.

I took another step away. "No, thank you. I've got to get—"

"I said why don't you sit back down," he commanded. "I'm not going to ask again." The music was loud but I managed to hear every word he said. I looked around the club but no one seemed to be paying any mind to this corner of the room.

I took a seat next to him. *Nico, help!* I was hoping he could hear me over the mass of people.

"Nico's been told to give us a few minutes, so I'll ask you not to speak to him right now and focus on me."

My head snapped sharply into focus. Shit. I was sitting next to another vampire. Someone who had the authority to tell Nico what to do. My nerves were starting to shake me. I nodded and looked over at the vampire. "Okay," I said, sitting back down beside him.

He turned his attention to me. "My name is Costin. I am the sovereign of the Toscana region." He looked over at me and realized that he had scared the shit out of me. "You do not need to fear me, I merely mean to speak with you so you and I can come to a better understanding of what it means to be a pet."

"It's a pleasure to meet you," I answered. I didn't know what else to say. It wasn't exactly every day I met a vampire, let alone one who ruled an entire region.

There was intelligence behind his eyes making him look older, but his skin was flawless. I studied him, realizing he looked younger than Nico by probably three or four years. Costin couldn't have been more than twenty six when he was turned. How many years ago was that?

Costin peered over me curiously as I sat tense beside him. He moved the collar of my shirt down, looking for something. Goosebumps covered me from neck to fingertips. "Has he not marked you yet?" His cold fingers pressed against my skin. "I can smell his scent on you, quite strong actually, but there is no mark." He made this more of an announcement than a question, but I still felt like he wanted an answer from me.

His comment about scent made me blush and I wasn't sure if he knew how the scent came to be. I prayed like hell he didn't.

The music continued to pound through the walls but it was as though someone had hit mute. I could only seem to focus on Costin and his intense stare. People walked past us, not looking twice. I wondered if Nico was watching us from another part of the club.

"I'm not sure what kind of mark you're looking for," I replied. I thought of the past forty eight hours and couldn't remember the word "mark" coming up in any of our conversations. There were much more interesting things to focus on which happened recently, I thought privately while replaying his caresses. I stopped suddenly and tried to think of anything but that in case Costin had the same ability to read minds as Nico. I focused on the music in the background and prayed that it was enough to mask any other thoughts I was having.

He let out a frustrated sigh. "The mark is as much to protect you as it is to make life easier on Nico. It marks you as his…staking his claim, if you will."

"What kind of mark?" I asked, instinctively placing a hand on my throat.

Costin nodded at my gesture. "Close. It is a bite mark, but it is something only other vampires will be able to see. Think of it as a black light sensitive stamp with a one-of-a-kind design. It is so other vampires do not try to attack you, or stake their own claim. It is against vampire law to kill the pet of another. Once you are the pet of one, you cannot belong to any other."

"So I need to be marked?" My voice caught on the words. I didn't like the idea of being bitten, but if it had to be done, I'd rather be claimed by Nico than someone else who wouldn't be gentle about it.

"You will be the first Nico has ever made, so it is vital both of you follow the rules. I will speak to him about this. You must be marked as soon as possible." He hesitated and his nostrils flared. "Though with his scent as strong as it is on you, I doubt there would be much confusion about whom you belong to."

I blushed automatically, knowing now he knew what the scent was. I wondered what he thought of that and wondered how much of the past few days he knew about. Had he ever done the same as Nico? Was he judging me as I sat here?

I felt very uncomfortable as Costin sat studying me. His gaze was almost palpable as it traveled the length of me. I waited for him to say something else, but we remained silent on the couch for several minutes.

"Do you have any questions for me?" He asked suddenly. He knew I did by the way he asked, his eyebrows raised.

Thinking for a minute, my mind spun out of control with the questions I could ask, including those that I was embarrassed to ask Nico or of which he refused to answer. But then again, I didn't really know Costin, either. There was no telling whether he would even answer my questions. I could get the same vague answers as I've been getting so far.

"No, not for now," I reached up and tightened my pony tail.

He bowed his head, accepting my answer. I had a million questions I refrained from asking and he knew it.

He finally moved by uncrossing his legs and taking my arm in his hand. He turned it over and slid his coarse hand down the entire length of my arm. He raised my wrist to his mouth and applied a small amount of pressure. I heard my breath catch as I watched him, afraid to panic. There was no sense in making a scene here if it wasn't necessary. He pressed his lips to the fast-beating pulse and then dropped my arm suddenly, "Be well, Dylan. We will see each other again soon, I am sure."

Costin was gone before I could look up. I took a deep breath and settled into the cushions of the couch as I tried to calm my breathing. My palms were sweaty and I pressed them to the fabric on my thighs to dry them and catch my breath. Nico walked around the corner with the wine glass that was now very much needed. He looked at me inquisitively as he sat down and handed me the Chianti.

"Wow," I breathed, reaching up with a shaky hand to grab the glass of wine.

"What did he say?" Nico settled next to me, his arm wrapping securely around my shoulders.

I brought the wine to my lips, drinking it faster than I

should have been. "You knew he was here? Did you know before you took me here?"

"Yes and no. He made himself known once we got here and I was told not to interfere." He leaned in closer.

"What was said? You look a little bit shaken."

I took another heavy sip. "That's putting it mildly. You couldn't hear?"

"Some," he admitted. "But it is difficult with this many people around." He leaned in close to me to have some privacy from anyone who could possibly overhear.

I swirled the wine in the glass and watched the red liquid slosh along the sides before it finally made it to my lips again.

He placed a hand over mine. "You may want to slow down," he whispered.

I took another sip, throwing caution to the wind. Finally, after yet one more sip, I set the glass down on the table in front of us. "He said you have to mark me."

Nico made a disgruntled face. "Yes – yes, I suppose I do. I was hoping to put it off for as long as possible."

"Why?" He didn't seem to want to do this, which confused me. Did he not want to make me his? Not that I was in any hurry to be bitten, but if even *he* wasn't looking forward to it, this was definitely not a good sign.

"You understand what the mark is, right? Costin

explained it to you?" Nico was looking stressed. The news of having to mark me was not sitting well with him.

I nodded. "It's a bite mark."

"Yes and no. I am afraid it is a little more complicated than what you think."

"You'll need to explain then." Sure, I'd read my share of fiction, but this was completely unfamiliar and I didn't understand what the big deal was.

"It is not just a bite. It is you giving yourself over to me, allowing me to claim you. We will form a bond that is beyond sinking my teeth into you. Our minds will synchronize, creating the mark that other vampires will be able to see. From what I hear, it is a very intimate transaction of faith."

It didn't make much sense to me, but then again, there was a lot of my new life that didn't make a whole lot of sense these days. "Okay, it sounds simple enough." I stared into his eyes and read the displeasure in them. There was obviously something here I wasn't getting. "So?"

"So I have to bite you – I have to drink blood from you," he paused and leaned in closer. "Which means I have to pull the willpower together to stop, which is always the most difficult part of sipping."

"Oh." It took me a second to process what he was saying. "Oh!" I gasped again. I looked at him, though, pressing my hand to the side of his face. "You can though, right?"

His eyes met mine and he covered my hand with his. "Of course, mia mortale. It is *you*, after all."

I smiled nervously. Of course he could.

Chapter 9

"YOU PROMISE TO actually answer some of my questions this time?" I asked, settling onto the red gingham plaid blanket Nico laid out on the grass.

He sat cross-legged on the blanket and had placed the basket in between us. He had packed it full for a picnic, despite the fact that it was one in the morning. "I do, but first you should eat something."

There were a few streetlights on the corner that strained to provide a decent amount of light into the waterfront park. Depending on the breeze that pushed through the trees, the light was just enough to make out both Nico's facial features and what was inside the basket.

Most of my meals lately seemed to consist of cherries, oranges, and anything else I'd use to garnish a drink at

Yankee Bar. But tonight, Nico was thoughtful and packed a basket full of snacks for me. I picked through the basket, finding a sandwich of questionable filling. It seemed that it was best not to ask when it came to Italian meats, I learned, so I plucked it out and bit into it. A small tremor shot through my jaw and made me realize just how hungry I was.

"So do I get to ask the questions?" I asked, leaning forward with my elbows on the wooden basket.

"You do. But can I ask a question first?"

I somehow knew what he was going to ask but I nodded, letting him go ahead.

"Will you be moving into your apartment sometime soon? You've had the key for almost a week."

Yep, I knew it. I had been putting it off for a while because, well, I didn't know. I was just nervous to take this next step, even though it wasn't as though I was living with Nico. Moving in to a permanent place was just so permanent. Although I knew I was staying, it wasn't a step I was quite ready to make yet, though it seemed as though there was no choice, not really.

"I'm paid on the hotel through tomorrow. I can move in tomorrow night, I guess."

Nico nodded his head. "Then it's settled. It's all taken care of and you have the address, yes?"

"Yes." The suitcases were piling up and my new

clothes were starting to cramp the small closet in a big way.

Nico watched me intensely as I picked through the basket and left part of the sandwich to the side. "You're hungry."

He said it as a statement, not a question.

I looked up at him because of the way he said it. "No," I said, trailing off. I was trying to be lady like but the truth was that ravenous was more of the word I would have used. "I just didn't get a chance to eat tonight – it was busy at the bar."

He let out a soft sigh. "Dylan, you can't starve yourself. You need to eat."

"And I am," I said, pulling out a bag of chips.

"Should I take you to a restaurant?" He started to rise. "Of course I should. How inconsiderate of me."

I rose to my knees and grabbed his hand. "Sit, I'm fine. You can buy me dinner tomorrow night when I don't have to work. You promised me answers tonight and that's all I'm really hungry for."

He shook his head to reprimand me in his own quiet way and let the subject drop away for a while.

The South Centro traffic was almost non-existent. Aside from a few cars passed along the main road periodically and the sound of my chips crunching, which suddenly sounded much louder than it should be, only the wind blowing through the trees that made any noise.

As the breeze made its way through the trees behind us, it let the lights on the riverfront illuminate our picnic a little more, allowing me to watch as Nico leaned on his side, his muscular arm folding to prop up his head.

"When are you going to mark me?" I asked suddenly. Costin made it sound important and Nico wasn't in too much of a hurry to heed his words. "Because Costin—"

"I know what he said, and soon. I want to make sure this is what you want before I claim you. You need to know the facts."

"Fair enough," I answered as I took the same position as Nico so I could watch the strands of his hair hang just over his forehead.

Nico pushed his hair back and licked his lips. "I suppose it's only right to start at the beginning. The history of our race is a little mixed. It started tens of thousands of years ago, before Christ was born. We are all descendants of one of five vampires, now known as the Imperial Five. It is believed that each of these five vampires came to be what they are through different means – witchcraft, sorcery and such. With each line of vampires, the changes are slightly different, though we all have the same basic weaknesses."

"Like sunlight?"

"Right. None of us can go out during the day,

however some of us transformed from human into vampire differently. Not everyone looks like me, mia mortale."

Goose bumps crossed my arms and a chill ran up my spine. "How do you mean?"

Nico stared off in the distance and twisted his mouth a couple times before answering. "It's hard to explain. I appear human, yes?"

I nodded.

"Not all vampires do. Some shift from human to vampire at will, leading them to appear very different in their vampire form. This can include claws, fangs, and various other changes. I have only met one other vampire line other than myself so I can only speak from what I know. The one vampire I met from another line looked much like myself with some slight differences. The other three lines of vampires are much rarer and it is more speculation on what makes them different than fact."

Different than human. Oh god. I pray I never meet one of those. The horror flicks I've seen growing up could have it right after all....

Nico focused in on me. "That's the history of us, though it can be confusing. Do you want to ask your questions to help clarify this or to make sense of the stories you've read?"

I wish I had written all the questions I had for him

down. Though he probably would have laughed. "If you were made from one line, then what happens if one of the Imperials dies?"

"Our blood bonds us together but it doesn't affect whether we live or die. My maker or one of the Imperials can pass and it wouldn't make a difference. I already have the blood coursing through me, therefore I can't die. The blood connects us in different ways, though. It allows us to communicate telepathically with each other. Once you are turned, you and I will be able to communicate just as I can with my maker."

"Is Costin your maker?"

"No. He is my sovereign only. I have taken a blood oath to him to be in his territory."

My eyes narrowed and I could feel a wrinkle forming across my forehead.

"This will make more sense in a year," Nico said, pushing the basket towards our feet, allowing us to close the distance between us a little easier. "For now, I can explain that there are sovereigns all over the world, keeping track of the vampire population in each city. We are led to believe that the Imperial Five appoint the sovereigns but Costin states he has never met any of them. He came into power because the previous sovereign ended his life and handed reign to him."

My fingers massaged my temples, trying to take all of

this in. "Okay, so how many sovereigns are there?"

"Two hundred or so." My eyes widened and he smirked. "Keep in mind that is across the globe. Some watch over three or four vampires, others watch over a hundred or so. It's to ensure no one creates too many more vampires and don't drain too much of the population."

I gasped at the thought. Innocent people's lives were at stake. Yet it didn't seem to matter, not really. The idea that people were dying so vampires could exist didn't seem tragic to me. Maybe it should have bothered me but it didn't. Cows and chickens die every year for humans. Vampires are simply higher up on the food chain.

"Then how many vampires are out there?" I asked. A car screeching around the corner snapped me out of my thoughts.

"No more than about a tenth of a percent of the human population – if a sovereign is doing his or her job. But this is across the globe. Tokyo and many larger cities have more. Otherwise, there is maybe only a handful here and there."

Did I even need to leave the United States to find a vampire?

On cue, he read my mind. "There are groups in the United States, but much smaller. Mainly in the Northeast. I'm glad you left to come here to find us." He leaned in to kiss me and pulled me by the hip to get me to scoot closer to him.

I gave in and closed the gap the rest of the way between us.

He licked over my lips, waiting to be invited in. I kept my mouth shut, toying with him. His lips twitched in a smile and I finally opened my mouth to give him access to delve in deeper. I let him taste me and explore me like he wanted. As my tongue fought his and traced his fangs, the taste of copper pennies overwhelmed my taste buds for a moment.

I pulled back. "When did you feed?"

Instinctively, he put his hand to his mouth. "You tasted blood?"

"I did."

"Right before I picked you up at the bar. Does it bother you?"

Nico seemed to tread lightly on this issue, not wanting to upset me. "No, it just surprised me."

He reached into the basket and pulled out a piece of chocolate, popping it in his mouth. "Better?" He raised an eyebrow.

He'd never eaten anything in front of me. The surprise must have been written across my face because his warm laugh suddenly filled the small space between us.

"I *can* eat. I just choose not to. Food cravings don't happen anymore."

"What else can you do? I mean, vampires," I wanted to get back to some of the questions I had for him while he was still willing to answer them.

"Well, vampires have basic skills. This includes the healing powers of the saliva and the mind control. As a vampire ages, they can pick up some additional skills. This can include flying and others. You will see soon enough what I am capable of."

Goose bumps traveled across my body. I already knew what he was capable of in one department, I thought to myself.

"What do you mean by mind control? Like when you take a sip from someone?"

Nico stretched, his slender frame arching and his arms coming down to rest by my head. "Yes. Some have stronger powers, though. I have known vampires who can lure victims to them. Then the victim goes back to their evening as though nothing ever happened."

First vampires are in the U.S. Then they can lure victims in? I could have been a victim without ever knowing it.

My face told too much, again. "You were never a vampire victim," Nico commented with amusement in his voice.

"You weren't. I'd sense it. Besides, most humans that survive these attacks are never quite the same again. The mind control can weaken the mind after a while, which is why we should never go after the same victim more than a few times. No matter how good they taste. Otherwise a sovereign steps in to handle the situation."

"And by handle you mean kill."

Nico nodded, watching my reactions to everything he said. To everything he explained. While I was glad I was getting the answers I've been waiting a lifetime to know, the way he kept saying 'human' made me all too aware that he and I were different in a way that was frightening and exhilarating at the same time.

"Do you have more questions for me?"

"One more," I admitted.

"Go ahead."

"Can you explain how you make me into a vampire yet?" The question has come up a few times and each time, he dismisses it completely.

He shook his head. "Not yet, *mia mortale*. Once you are marked, then I will be able to discuss more with you. But only then."

"Okay," I said, settling in, slightly annoyed that I couldn't get all my questions answered.

Nico sensed I was disappointed. "Come closer," he tugged at my hips to bring me against him. As I moved in to an intimate distance, I knew all too well why he fed before picking me up. It was pressed into my belly, sending butterflies swirling into my stomach and much lower.

He effortlessly rolled me over so his body was pinned over mine. I laughed lightly and delighted in the strength of his body. Pools of royal blue stared down at me. His tongue traced the lines of my lips and my hands went to the back of his neck.

"Mmmm," I moaned into his ear, nibbling on his lobe a little.

"That's it." His hand was halfway under my shirt when I felt his entire body tense.

"Don't move," he mouthed to me.

"What's the matter?" I whispered almost inaudibly.

He pressed a finger to my lips to quiet me. "We are not alone."

My eyes grew wide as I stared up at him. I was afraid to breathe, let alone to look past him and see what had him so uneasy. Nico didn't seem thrilled about his findings so I remained quiet and pondered if I would regret looking up.

Nico remained tense above me, though I could feel he was ready to spring up if the situation called for it.

"Do. Not. Move," he warned, sensing I grew impatient under him.

I simply nodded, not knowing what else I could do.

Chapter 10

"DOESN'T THIS LOOK cozy," a strange voice sounded several feet away.

I was trying to figure out who this intruder was and why he was bothering us. It didn't seem like Nico to react so quickly to someone unless this wasn't just any intruder. I was waiting for something to happen because I was convinced that our not-so-friendly intruder was a vampire, too. It was the only reason Nico would get so tense so quick.

"Dylan, it's good to see you again, though I must say, I'm a bit jealous."

He peered over at the same moment I mustered the nerve to glance in his direction. His dark blonde hair hung loose in a tousled mess, parted slightly to the side. He had sideburns that extended down his high cheekbones and then disappeared into a close-shaven beard. A white t-shirt clung to his chest and let me know that he was muscular. His chocolate brown eyes stared at me intensely as I fought to look away.

Nico jumped to his feet and pulled me up as well. "Do you know him?" Nico asked, glancing from me to our fair haired guest.

I shook my head. "No." I wanted to make it a question because while his voice sounded vaguely familiar, I stared at the tall vampire with black tattoos covering his forearms and saw only a stranger.

"The girl is mine. Please leave and we won't have to argue about this." Confidence resonated from the stranger and he spoke matter-of-factly.

Nico stood up in a single movement. "I don't know who you are, but no, she does not belong to you. I have already claimed her."

"She is yours then?"

"I have already said she is."

The over confident stranger took a few steps towards us and crunched the dry grass as he walked. "Then you wouldn't mind me looking for a mark?"

My mind raced. A mark. *The* mark. The one I didn't have yet – the one coming any day…if only I had insisted a little more. If only Costin had insisted a little more. Who was this guy, anyway?

Nico took a step forward. "I said she was mine."

The voice laughed arrogantly. "You haven't marked her yet." He made this a statement, not a question. He didn't need to step any closer because he knew he wasn't going to find a mark.

I was certain that I had never laid eyes on him before. I would have remembered a face like that. Still, I couldn't shake a feeling of déjà vu. His eyes remained focused on me and the hair on every part of my body bristled. I knew him from somewhere, but the face staring back at me was completely foreign. I kept going through the different people I met at the bar the other night. Could I have served him a drink? How could he possibly want to stake claim on someone he's never even met?

"Dylan." The accent was familiar, but it wasn't Italian. As I played the sound back in my head repeatedly, I finally realized where the accent was from. Paris.

He watched my face as my mind worked to solve the puzzle. "Ahh, then you do remember me," he stated, stepping towards me, a smile curving out of the corner of his mouth.

Nico stepped in between the two of us to block my view of this man. "She doesn't seem too thrilled about it, either."

"We'll see about that," the voice sounded again. He peered around Nico to look at me. "The name is Olivier." He extended his hand out to mine in greeting. I just stared at it. "We hadn't had a chance to meet properly at the Place de la Bastille."

My attention focused on at Nico, wondering how to proceed. Did Nico understand this is what scared me into leaving France early and Olivier had stalked me across several countries?

Olivier began to close the gap between us. "You smell of him," he announced, almost surprised. He glanced at Nico and back at me as he contemplated his previous statement. "Impressive. I've yet to have a human survive my efforts. You must be stronger than you look."

It took me a moment to figure out what he was talking about until I saw the way he was sizing me up. My breath caught in my chest and my pulse sped.

Nico caught my eye and mouthed, "Run."

Before I could make sense of anything or ask questions, like where was I supposed to go, my mind took hold and I ran. I darted across the lawn to nowhere in particular. The streets of Santa Croce seemed like a logical place to start. I heard snarling behind me and knew that they were fighting. I wanted to turn around to see who was winning. I couldn't risk it, so I kept running. I raced past the looming trees of the park and into the quiet streets.

I had to have faith Nico would take care of Olivier, the very man who had stalked me in a street in Paris and scared me to the very core. I knew I hadn't exaggerated my fear that night. I just couldn't see anything. It was one thing to think you're being followed and another to have it confirmed.

I thought about what Nico had said about mind control and not knowing about being a vampire victim and shuddered. Olivier could have attacked me without me ever recalling it. Despite knowing that my safety had remained intact while in Paris didn't allow me to forget that it was gone now.

I heard more noises behind me and I turned around to see them wrestling through the park. A picnic bench was knocked over and if they weren't careful, trees were going to be next. Their movements were so fast it was difficult to make out the blurs. While I was able to catch the blue of Nico's shirt and then the white of Olivier's, it was impossible to know who was doing the most damage. I turned around to ensure no one was witness to what was going on. The crash of their bodies sounded into the night. To anyone who was listening, it would simply sound like thunder. They pushed through the park, rustled foliage, and continued to beat on each other. I sensed that each was taking their turn giving and receiving blows and knew there would be residual damage in the morning.

There were no bystanders. I was alone with the battle behind me. There was nowhere to run. While I knew Olivier would find me eventually, I couldn't stand around and wait for him. I ran in hopes of coming up with a plan to save myself and help Nico.

Olivier could take me because I wasn't marked. I kept running but my legs were quickly defying me, cramping at the calf and slowing me down. I cursed and doubled over on the street, huffing in an attempt to secure my breathing. My lungs were burning and I knew I wasn't going to be able to run anymore. I could still hear the thunder of the fight yet it was too far back to see it anymore.

I wiped the sweat from my forehead with the back of my hand, closing my eyes to think. Where was I going to go? How far could I get before the two of them were done? Even if they could go on for hours, dawn would show up eventually. They would have to quit soon, whether they were done or not. My hotel was an option, though I didn't know if it was truly safe. I needed a safeguard and thought about what would protect me. Holy water? A cross? These were questions I should have been asking a while ago.

I wondered how to get ahold of Costin. He would know how to get Nico and me out of this mess. Slowly, I stood up again, stretching my legs to give them some relief. I wanted to shout his name, hoping he'd hear me and come to my aid. Common sense told me I couldn't do that. Someone would hear me and wonder what the hell I was doing.

Then I remembered Nico wasn't the only one who could read my mind. *Costin...Costin...Costin...* I walked through the city repeating his name in my head in hopes that he was listening. I felt ridiculous being unable to let anything else cross my mind except for his name. He would have to hear it eventually, even if I had to cover every inch of this city. Even if he didn't hear the message, one of the others would and tell him that I needed assistance. *Costin! I need to speak with you!*

I strained to hear the quarrel. It was no longer audible and knew it wasn't a good sign. I knew Nico was strong, though that came with the territory of being a vampire. Olivier could be just as strong or stronger. Olivier could be older or younger than Nico, too. Visually, he couldn't have been more than a few years, but in vampire years it could be a hundred years or more. I didn't want to lose him for so many reasons.

***

I was tired and my legs were barely able to keep me

moving. I'd been walking and running off and on for what seemed like hours with no sign of anyone. I had crossed the bridge and was now closer to my hotel, which was drawing me in because exhaustion was setting in.

Neither vampire had come looking for me, for which I was thankful at least one of them hadn't found me again. What was going to happen to Nico? I needed some help with this situation. I felt as if I were in unchartered waters.

I continued down the roads ultimately leading to the hotel and passed a late-night pizzeria. I paid the few college students sitting outside eating pizza no mind and continued around the next bend. A door to a pub swung open and nearly hit me.

"Get in here," a voice laced with irritation commanded.

I stopped short and looked up to see Costin holding the door. The pub was crowded and the loud music was drowning out all conversations.

"Now," he said prior to walking into a back room beyond the layers of smoke without waiting for me. I followed at once. No one from the crowds of people tore attention away from their beer bottles and cigarettes. At last, he sat at a tall bar stool in a semi-quiet corner.

"Why have you been looking for me tonight and where's Nico?"

I took a deep breath. He certainly didn't make it easy to talk to him. He was pretty intimidating. "I'm sorry, I didn't know who else to turn to. Another vampire apparently had seen me when I was in Paris. He found Nico and I at the waterfront park earlier."

"And…?" Costin asked, trying to get me to make my point faster.

"Well," I continued, trying to figure out how to say all of this. Costin wasn't the easiest person to talk to, but I had no choice since Nico was the only other person I really knew here. "This other vampire is trying to claim me."

"But he can't."

I didn't want to tell Costin that I wasn't marked. After the first meeting with him, I knew it was important. Unfortunately for me, it wasn't as important to Nico for one reason or another.

Understanding flashed across his face. "Nico hasn't marked you." His annoyance at me not being marked yet was evident.

I nodded.

Costin pounded his fist onto the table and caused it to shake back and forth. "Damn it."

"That's putting it mildly," I said dryly.

"So what happened next?"

"I don't know. Nico told me to run and I heard them

fighting...."

I paused, struggling with the words to describe what just transpired.

Before I could go any further, Costin was gone. I glanced awkwardly to see if anyone noticed how he just seemed to vanish, but everyone continued drinking and laughing and carrying on. *Okay, then. I hope that helped.*

I stood up and made my way out of the place.

For the second time in one night, I wandered the streets aimlessly without direction. I could return to the park to see what was going on between Nico, Olivier, and now Costin, or I could get the hell out of dodge. Leaving town seemed like a quick fix but I didn't know where I would go and didn't want to leave Nico behind.

Olivier would most likely find me no matter where I ended up. I couldn't go anywhere without knowing where Nico was and if he was safe. Who knew what Olivier was capable of? Nico could be in just as much danger as I was. Costin seemed pissed and he could very well take that anger out on Nico for not following a direct order to mark me.

I knew one thing for sure: I was not safe. Obviously, Olivier had some really good tracking skills to be able to follow me all the way from Paris, so running seemed pointless. After a while of debating, I decided to go back to where it all began.

The park was vacant of any life, or afterlife. Tall grass and the upturned park bench were the only things visible. The thundering sounds from before had subsided and I strained to hear something. I focused every cell in my body, listening for someone, as I approached the waterfront. I saw the blanket we had laid out earlier, which was now just a trampled pile of fabric. Other than that, there was no sign of the vampires anywhere.

"Nico?" I called, just a little over an audible whisper.

Nothing.

"Anyone?" I tried again, just a little louder.

Still nothing.

I wandered the waterside for another hour, waiting for someone to get me. I jumped at every sound the park made, including crickets, birds, and a dog barking in the distance, though nothing else of importance. I finally sat on the bench to sit. I dozed off a few times, waking only to watch the bright oranges and pinks fill the sky as the sun rose and realized no one was coming for me and that I had no clue where Nico was and if he was hurt

I was alone.

Chapter 11

MY SUITCASES WERE packed, standing next to the door of the hotel room. I sat on the bed and held the key Nico had given me as I read the address over and over again. I hadn't heard from him in over twenty four hours, which wasn't like him, or from Costin and Olivier. I was thankful for the latter.

There was nothing to do but move into the apartment. At least I would feel closer to Nico until I could actually figure out where the hell he and Costin went. This trip to Florence was scaring the hell out of me because I couldn't go home and suddenly I found myself very alone. Nico was my only link in this city and he had to turn up sooner rather than later.

A knock at the door broke my thoughts. Room

service – a young boy with a cart was letting me know the taxi I had called had arrived, and he would help me down with my bags. I had spent plenty of my money at this hotel, so it was time to give this apartment across town a shot. Nico had paid for it so it was the least I could do.

The hotel attendant was dressed in a ridiculous little red suit, complete with a hat with brass buckles. If I weren't confident that this was his first job, I would have laughed outright. He loaded my bags up carefully, checking the room to see if I was alone. He was probably wondering why I had come alone, or why I needed all of these bags for one person. I took a quick inventory of the room to make sure I wasn't missing anything. I nodded to him and we worked our way down the hall to the elevator.

The taxi ride was pleasant enough, though traffic was heavy and my driver liked to use his horn a lot. About ten minutes later, we passed the entrance to the Boboli Gardens, where Nico and I had our first kiss.

I placed my hand to my lips and remembered that kiss as if it had taken place just moments ago. Just over a day without Nico had passed and I was already missing him. I wondered if he was okay or if Olivier had hurt him. My mind raced with a hundred different possibilities of what *could* have happened. I had thought the whole idea of tracking Costin down was to get some answers, though he, too, had vanished and left me without any answers at all.

The palazzo where my apartment was stood three stories high. It was a yellowish-gold building with high arches and an unidentifiable charm. I paid my taxi driver and dragged three suitcases up a winding flight of stairs to my apartment. *My apartment*…it still didn't sound real. I tripped over a suitcase and cursed the fact that, like so many of these old buildings, there was no elevator. I got to the third level and saw the door to my place. The key turned easily enough and I pushed the door open. I looked around to find it was completely furnished, as promised, in a very modern style. It looked as though it leapt from the pages of an Ikea catalog or a home fashion magazine. I was impressed

If Nico expected me to feel comfortable, he definitely did a good job. There was no way that I would have to do any remodeling. Silver mirrors lined the entry way, which led into the living area where a deep red sofa with over-stuffed pillows sat. Gray-hued frames depicting landscapes of Florence from centuries ago clung to the walls. Striped wallpaper lined the dining room, where a large oak table filled the vast space. Light wood was my style, so I was beyond pleased that he had done so well decorating. I had a sneaking suspicion that Nico had done some research somehow to find out what I liked. As soon as I found him, I would have to thank him for giving me such an amazing apartment to call home.

I walked into the bedroom and instantly fell in love. The bedroom was not only spacious, it had a large canopy bed that filled the room so well. There were tons of pillows stacked against the headboard and I couldn't wait for nightfall in order to sink into them. I flopped down across the bed for a moment to relax and gather my thoughts.

I was alone again. That wasn't the part bothering me, since I came to Florence alone. Things were much different than they were two and a half weeks ago. It seemed longer, like it should have been months, but life had been in fast-forward since I met Nico. Even if I wanted to go back to Florida, I couldn't with all this new information. Life was different…my whole world had been turned upside down and it wasn't something I was willing to just ignore.

I had met a vampire, which was my goal of this trip, no matter how much I played it off that it wasn't. I hadn't figured on falling for one, though. I was to be marked and made into one, since I was allowed to live with the truth. I couldn't wait for Nico to show up again, though I was thankful that the bar could occupy at least some of the time in between waiting. I had the utmost faith in Costin. He couldn't have become sovereign without being a responsible leader. It was taking much longer than anticipated, though.

If Nico and Costin didn't show up sometime in the

near future, it begged the question of what would happen next. If another vampire knew about me, would I still be required to be marked? Time would tell. I was sure that other vampires knew of my existence. I seemed to be the only mortal one in the group and word had probably traveled about Nico and I.

One of the vampires had to know how to get ahold of their sovereign, though I had no idea how to get ahold of one of them. I would give it a few more days or nights to see how things played out.

The apartment was quiet. I couldn't hear the traffic outside or any tourists afoot. A soft hum came from the refrigerator and the bed creaked slightly when I got up and that was it. I followed the humming into the kitchen to see if Nico had remembered that I was human and needed to eat something.

I smiled as I found the refrigerator was stocked more than was necessary. It had a variety of everything, including sodas, waters, cheeses, meats, and snacks. There was so much inside that it was hard to decide what to have first.

I grabbed a bottle of water and a few slices of salami. As I shut the door, I found a piece of paper taped to the front. I hadn't seen it before, but it was a note, folded over. I shoved the salami in my mouth and sat up on the kitchen counter to read.

Nico's cursive was scrawled across the paper.

Mia Mortale –

Trust me when I say I am fine. Costin has gone to get the help of some nearby sovereigns as Olivier has proven to be stronger than either of us would have imagined. He is smitten with you and won't back down. Our only hope now is to get you and I alone long enough to mark you. Not the romantic time I would have wanted, but it is now a matter of keeping you safe. I will contact you again soon.

Nico.

My heartbeat sped up just being able to read something from Nico to let me know he was okay. I read the note several times before folding it back up. Olivier was smitten with me? I wondered how much danger that put Nico into and how they were going to get nearby sovereigns involved. It also concerned me that Nico was leaving out some important information – he tended to do that when he thought it would upset or worry me. I cursed myself for picking Paris to go to first. If I had just come to Italy first, none of this would have ever happened. *But it did, so now what?*

I would just have to wait for Nico to contact me again. It started to make sense. That was why the refrigerator was so well stocked. Nico didn't want me to leave the apartment. I wondered how he was able to get into the apartment without Olivier seeing him. I knew they each probably had their own different strengths or powers or whatever, but still. Mind control didn't work on other vampires, did it? I doubted it, which means that maybe, just maybe, Costin was able to help throw Olivier off my scent for a little while.

I looked at my watch and realized that it was time to get ready for work. Maybe this was the distraction I needed. I thought about calling in, but when I thought about what was waiting for me in some of the stores in Tornabuoni, I realized how badly I wanted the money to get some new things for my closet. I could probably ask Nico to buy things for me, but it would be more satisfying if I took care of it on my own. Walking over to the bar would take me a little longer from here than from the hotel, though.

After getting my makeup on and a gray pin-stripe vest on over my black pants, I was ready to go. Walking there wasn't bothering me because it was still light out. I wondered if I could talk Matt, Giancarlo, or one of the servers to walk me home after we closed? Would it put them in danger, too?

***

"Ciao," I said, walking in the employee entrance at

Yankee. I saw Giancarlo was working with me again tonight and he was already cutting fruit for the garnish station so I jumped behind the bar to start stocking the beer cooler.

He gave me a nod and kept on cutting limes. He wasn't very talkative until he took a few shots Matt wasn't supposed to know about right before the rush hit. I was happy to see Giancarlo tonight because he was as outgoing as I was behind the bar, which was great because it helped fill up the tip jar quicker, too.

Like I suspected, we were getting low on Red Bull, so I added it to the list of things to get from the back.

"So you can pretty much drop a shot of anything into the Red Bull and people will drink it, yeah?" Giancarlo asked.

I laughed. Sounds like he's been experimenting while I've been gone. "Yeah. It's popular, isn't it?"

I grabbed my list and headed to the walk in cooler in the kitchen. As I was walking back out with a case in tow, Matt caught up to me.

"You were right," he said, following me through the dining room. "We went through a case and a half the other night. I got a few more cases in, but they go quicker when you or Giancarlo are here. Are you sure I can't convince you to pick up a few more shifts? I mean, you can't tell me three shifts a week is enough to keep your finances afloat, right?"

I could tell the urgency in his voice for me to agree to

more nights, but I had enough on my plate right now.

I shook my head. "I'd love to help you out, I just can't right now." I hoisted the case on top of the bar and Giancarlo grabbed it to bring over to the other side.

"Okay. Just let me know if you change your mind. The offer stays on the table." Matt walked back to the dining room and started to gather up some of the servers for a meeting and I went back behind the bar.

I went through a mental list of everything I needed around me tonight. I was ready for the rush and was happy to have the distraction in front of me so I could take a breather from the past twenty-four hours of stress. I watched as Matt opened the doors and pushed vampire politics to the back of my mind as the bar started to fill up.

Giancarlo downed two shots of whiskey and I saw the smile appear on his face almost instantly. He glanced sideways at me and knew he was ready. I gave him a nudge with my elbow and smiled. "You ready?"

"Oh yeah," he responded, pulling out his lighter from his back pocket. "Let's do this."

Within moments, the bar was full with hands waving Euros in front of us and shouting drinks over masses of people.

Matt came over to me after locking the front door. I

was perched on the edge of the bar, downing a bottle of water after a crazy night. "Good night?" he asked.

"Very," I commented. "Thanks."

He pushed his hair out of his face. "You and Giancarlo make a good team. I wish all my bartenders got into the flair like the two of you. I've never seen a show like what you guys do."

I smiled. It was true. He and I really got a large crowd going. My days of bartending years ago paid off. I enjoyed nights where I reveled in the crowds and just mindlessly poured drinks and twirled bottles. "I'm still not picking up another shift for you."

"Was I that obvious?" He smiled and attempted to use his schoolboy good looks to charm me.

I nodded, jumping down from the bar. "I'm gonna get out of here. I'll see you on Saturday."

Maria, who was one of the servers, was leaving as I did. She was a little flaky but friendly nonetheless. I walked with her a few blocks and talked to her about nothing in particular. I know I shouldn't be walking alone at night so some company was better than nothing. Her English wasn't great, but as I looked at the tight shirt across her chest, I knew she wasn't hired for her great conversational skills.

As I walked the last few blocks in the dark by myself, my heart sped a little more, anticipating something. When a bird chirped, I jumped. My eyes were glued to every moving object and anything that lurked in the shadows. Not that I knew what would happen if something did jump out at me, yet I prepared myself nonetheless.

Luckily, nothing came of it. Costin must have resolved everything as he had promised.

Chapter 12

AS I CLIMBED the stairs to my apartment, I began to relax again.

I walked in the front door, noticing it was unlocked. A smile spread across my face, quickening my pace just a little, "Nico," I called.

The bathroom door opened and steam poured out.

"Nico," I called again, getting excited and doing everything but run to the entrance of the bathroom. "I'm so glad—"

"Dylan."

"You're—!" I gasped "You're not Nico."

I exhaled slowly and took a step back and my nerves kicked into high gear. Olivier stood in the doorway with his dark blonde hair wet and slicked back against his head. He wore nothing but one of my oversized cotton towels and a smirk.

Everything in my being told me to run, but knew it would do no good. This was a dangerous man. Nico and Costin struggled with him and his power radiated off of him.

Not knowing whether to scream or run, I just stood there, staring at his sculpted abs glistening with water and the trail of dark hair that crept beneath the towel.

The thought to run was becoming stronger but moving wasn't happening. I took a step backwards and tried to avert my attention to anything other than his glistening biceps painted with tribal tattoos.

I let out a startled gasp as he moved in on me.

"Dylan," he called out. "I thought you'd like this. Perhaps my introduction in the park was too aggressive."

My heart was in my throat and my mouth went dry. I couldn't seem to find enough voice to say anything.

"Do you not like what you see?" He asked, his voice playing with the very root of what made me female. It didn't matter if he was a vampire or what his intentions were. It's hard to keep my mind in the game when I'm staring at over six feet of chiseled perfection in Egyptian cotton less than an arm's length reach away.

I was hoping like hell that Costin or Nico would jump in at any time. I took another step back and shook my head slightly from side to side. I didn't want to *say* anything. My voice would betray me in one way or another. I certainly didn't want to *do* anything, either, especially not what Olivier had in mind.

"Dylan, come now," he cooed as he walked towards me. "You can't possibly want him over me. I'm younger, much closer to your age. Besides, I'm a better kisser."

"I-I...." I stammered with words and fell into the chair in an effort to dodge him. "I'm not—"

"Interested? I think you are. I think you just need a little convincing." He grabbed me by the shoulders, pulling me out of the chair.

His arms wrapped in front of me, pressing him more intimately to my backside than I thought ever imaginable. I fought to get out of his grip and he strengthened his hold on me. I was vaguely aware that my squirming was arousing him more than it was allowing me to get loose. He was very interested, judging by the pressure that was getting firmer against me.

"Hold still!" He pulled my hair with considerable force.

"What do you want from me?" I asked, trying to pull free, though I knew it was pointless. No amount of strength I could ever muster would be enough to get myself loose from Olivier. It was like being held in place by concrete.

"It's not obvious?" He pulled me closer to him, if it was even possible.

Oh, it's obvious, I thought. I squirmed against him in an effort to get an inch between us.

His breath crept across my skin as he inhaled and exhaled. "You smell really good. No wonder Niccolò can't keep his hands off you."

"Please," I begged. I found myself wishing for a few things – like not coming home alone and for shorter hair. He gripped a good handful of it to keep me taut against him.

"We need to talk."

"About what?"

"Everything."

"I have nothing to say to you."

He didn't like my answers and he pulled my wrists tighter into his grip. My wrists were pinned to my side with his right hand when I saw the door to the balcony open.

Two figures walked in – Costin and a new guy, someone I didn't recognize. The stranger had jet black hair hanging loose past his shoulders. His skin was a little darker, maybe of Hispanic origin. His eyes were the same shade of black as his hair and he stared at me through loose strands, which hung in his way.

"Costin!" I shouted.

Costin looked over at me and gave me a nod, as if to

say not to worry.

"Tell them to leave," Olivier said.

"No."

"Olivier, just let her go," he commanded, crouching in his tan slacks, ready to attack.

There was a laugh echoing through my ear. "Why would I do that? I just got her where I want her." He slid his hand over my head and smoothed my hair under his palm.

I wiggled against his embrace as he stood there, locking me in his grasp. Costin better have another plan than just asking nicely.

"She's not yours," the stranger spoke, mirroring the fighting stance Costin had taken on the other side of us.

Were they going to fight in my apartment? While I knew they didn't want any witnesses, the square footage of my place was limited.

I took the opportunity to pull against Olivier when I felt his grip go slack on me. As soon as he felt me move, I was pinned to him even tighter.

"Keep wiggling," he whispered in my ear. "It feels wonderful."

Ugh. I stopped wiggling instantly to ensure that I wasn't going to give him the satisfaction of getting off on my struggles.

"She. Is. Not. Yours," the stranger emphasized again.

Olivier turned to address the men. "That's where we disagree. I saw her weeks ago. She was mine then and she's mine now. She disappeared out of Paris quicker than I anticipated, though, and it took me a little while to track her down." He grabbed my hair again, bringing my head against his. I let out a yelp of pain before I could muffle it. "You just had to check out early, didn't you?"

This information caught me off guard. Had he known when I was supposed to check out from my hotel? The idea of him getting any personal information of mine made me cringe when the dark haired vampire to my left let out a deep-throated snarl. It startled me back, closer to Olivier, which was the last thing I had wanted. I was hoping the stranger wasn't going to attack Olivier while I was standing in his arms.

"Easy, precious," Olivier whispered to me. "I won't let any harm come to you." He stroked my hair as his hand made its way up the back of my neck.

I shivered uneasily. Part of me was waiting for Nico to come down into the balcony at any moment and save me from this. I stared at the empty balcony and then back at the scene before me. Shit, I wasn't going anywhere anytime soon.

"You can't mark her, so what's your plan?" Costin demanded. He had stood up and was leaning against the couch, almost nonchalantly.

"And why can't I?" Olivier asked, amusement in his tone.

"She has to pledge herself to you, and she won't do that," Costin said. "You know the rules."

Olivier seemed to think about this for a moment. "Why wouldn't she pledge herself to me?" He looked over at Costin and then to the stranger, as if daring them to go up against him. "Besides, you know what they say about rules."

I finished the thought for him – they were made for breaking. If he was going to break rules, though, I was screwed. My only hopes were that Nico was making a hell of a lot better progress than Costin was.

"What makes you think I'd pledge myself to you?" I asked vehemently.

He laughed against my ear again. "Why wouldn't you?"

The man was so cocky that it pissed me off. Before I could start naming off the reasons, the stranger stepped in. "You can't use mind control to sway her decisions. Marking must be a two-sided decision and she has already pledged herself to Nico."

Wait a second...mind control? I thought that was for making people forget or getting them to do something, not controlling feelings. Could Olivier use mind control to make me want him? I was hoping the answer was no, but as I read the concern across Costin's face, I wasn't so sure. I stood completely pinned and unable to do anything but verbally object to whatever might come my way. This was so *not* how I pictured the evening going when I came home.

"Prove I used mind control as I mark her, gentlemen," Olivier dared. As I felt his breath on my neck, I was regretting wearing the vest tonight. At least something with a collar would have protected me a little bit more for a few seconds, at least. The strength in his grasp made me think of something he had said to me earlier. He was younger than Nico. I knew Nico was over two hundred years old, but with my eyes shut their strength mirrored each other. That begged the question of how much younger was Olivier than Nico? More importantly, how bad could this be for me?

He drew me in closer and licked the nape of my neck before turning me around so I was peering into his deep blue eyes. My body cringed at the sensation of his fingers on my hairline and I moved my head. I did not want to look into his eyes. He took my face in both of his hands and placed his icy palms on my cheeks. They were colder than Nico's. I hoped it wasn't because Olivier hadn't fed recently.

"Dylan," he said low into my ear. "Look at me."

His voice echoed inside my head and I looked at him. His gaze bore into mine like two amber gems.

"Good girl," he commended.

He continued focusing on me and holding my head in his hands so I had no choice but to lock into his stare. I could always shut my eyes, but I didn't trust anyone on the balcony, so I kept them open. Who knows what could happen if I closed them for longer than a blink?

Olivier breathed in my scent and smiled. "Dylan, I want you."

I obeyed, pressing my body against his. We never looked away from each other and yet my actions were not my own. I didn't enjoy the proximity to him, but I felt completely incapable of doing anything to my own accord. Just as I was thinking it, the stranger spoke.

"Costin, you must do something. He already has her under his control."

Costin nodded. "It took less time than I thought it would."

I was trapped inside my body, hearing their words and wanting to say or do something, but my fears had come true. Olivier had me under his control.

The smell of Olivier was much different in comparison to Nico. His breath was like spearmint. The intoxicating smell was lingering in front of me and calling to me. It made me want nothing more than to taste his mouth to see if coincided with the smell. That would do it. A long, sensual kiss from the sexy man in front of me would help to cure any curiosity that I had.

I looked up at Olivier and licked my lips slowly and purposefully, never backing down from him. The corners of his mouth turned upwards in a smile. It wasn't long before his lips started to inch towards mine, though it seemed like an eternity before they would meet.

Around us, the earth seemed to stand still. There was just Olivier and me. A light humming sound encompassed us in our own little bubble. There was stubble on Olivier's chin and I reached out to run my fingers along it in hopes of bringing his mouth closer to mine faster.

"That's it, love," Olivier said softly. "Focus on me. Bring me your lips. I cannot wait to taste them."

The stranger tried to step in between Olivier and me but Olivier had his hand up, sending some kind of electric charge at him.

"What the -," Costin asked, bewildered by what just happened.

The stranger shook his head, confused by the situation as well.

"Fight it, Dylan," Costin yelled in the background, but I couldn't seem to find the meaning of what he was saying. Fight what? Why would I want to fight this gorgeous creature?

Olivier's thumbs rubbed along my jaw line as he held

my head steady in his grip. The chill in his hands left a numbing sensation across my skin and I felt like gelatin in his arms. I couldn't think about anything else except the distance his lips were from mine and the strong desire to close the gap.

I raised myself on tiptoe to compensate for his height.

Olivier watched me closely and his lips moved epically slow towards mine. He brought his right hand to rest on my hip while his other hand guided my face towards him. He tilted my head to one side, exposing the full length of my neck to him. His head bowed nearer to my skin and I could feel my heart beat faster as his breath left cold, tingling sensations through me.

His eyes gleamed a dozen different shades of blue. I watched only him as the other men seemed to blur into the background.

"Do you want me?"

I nodded. The sound of his voice was like velvet. His words were like unspoken promises of all the ways he could pleasure me.

"Let me hear you say it."

"I want you." There wasn't anything in the world that I wanted more. This man was the embodiment of sex and lust and everything else. I wanted him, plain and simple.

"Dylan, you must pay attention!" Costin screamed.

He came into focus and before I could ask what he meant, he lunged towards us.

Costin's entire weight came crashing into me. This started a chain reaction where Olivier staggered backwards and had no choice but to release his grip on me. I fell into the chair, which quickly tipped over with my weight. I then found myself on the floor, sprawled awkwardly with my feet on top of the chair.

I blinked, taking a moment to realize what was going on.

Olivier was composing himself and quickly looked over at me. He leaned past Costin to try and meet my gaze.

What the hell was he about to do? I looked back at Costin and the stranger. I scooted out of the chair the rest of the way and over to the wall, my feet out in front of me. "What's going on?" I could not read the look of determination on Olivier's face.

"Fight it," Costin ordered as he crouched by Olivier.

"How?"

Costin looked over at me but said nothing. He didn't know. I was convinced of it. I had a feeling it had to do with the electric spark that Olivier had sent out, but couldn't be sure. Had he known how to fight it, he would have told me or at least have done something to help.

Mind control. It hung in my head like a flashing neon

light. How could I fight something like this? A minute ago I had actually wanted Olivier to kiss me. Would it have been enough of an invitation for him to mark me? I blinked again and shook my head to clear my thoughts. My mind was racing in a thousand directions when a slap across my face stung me back into reality.

"Focus, love," Olivier shouted. My cheek was still burning as I stared up at him. "You are mine. Do you not want me?"

I closed my eyes, trying not to pay him any mind or let him bring me under again. "No, I don't," I said defiantly, my eyes still squeezed shut.

I heard laughing behind me. Costin and the stranger were laughing at my comment to Olivier, which was enough to distract him. The stranger jumped in front of Olivier and pulled me into his arms. He ran out the door of the balcony and jumped with me still in tow. Just as we disappeared into the night, I watched Costin descend on Olivier, fangs exposed in such a ghastly display. I was glad not to be around to watch what happened next.

To say we were flying may be the wrong words, but we were in the air. We were above the city by several hundred feet, unbeknownst to the residents and tourists below. The wind was cold and so were the arms wrapped around me. The stranger whose arms I was in was obviously a friend of

Costin, though at this point, I wasn't sure whom I could trust. I was away from Olivier though, so I should at least take comfort in that.

We landed a few minutes later, on the roof of a palazzo just south of the Arno. I locked eyes with my savior, still in awe of how it was we arrived here.

He smiled and set me down to get on my own two feet. "I'm Pablo," he announced, a rich Spanish accent evident in those simple words. Pablo pushed his hair out of his face and sat next to me on the terracotta tiles of the roof.

I gestured to myself, "I'm assuming I don't need an introduction."

"No, you don't. Costin came to visit me in Barcelona last night to help the three of you out with your…admirer."

I wasn't amused. "Admirer. Yes, well, that's certainly one way to describe Olivier. Where is Nico? Is he okay?"

"He is fine. He's in Paris right now trying to track down the sovereign there."

"How long will that take?"

Pablo shrugged. "I'm not sure. We are hoping it will only take another night."

"What is the plan? I mean, we can't wait around for another attack. Is there anything I can do to help? I know I'm not as strong as all of you, but…"

"There is nothing for you to do. You have stayed

alive thus far and you are doing just fine. Allow us to protect you until you become marked."

"When will that be?" I asked, rocking slowly, trying to calm all of my nerves at once, which wasn't working. I felt like I needed a bottle of wine and a way to erase my mind of the past hour. People bustled below me, talking and laughing. They were completely unaware of the actions which had taken place. Maybe ignorance was bliss.

Pablo turned to me, placing an arm on my shoulder. "Well, I've been asked to mark you myself if it comes to it. However, Nico should be back before it is necessary."

"*You'll* mark me?" I asked. This was not what I agreed to – I wanted Nico, not someone else. I didn't even know this Pablo. Besides, was it Costin or Nico who asked him to mark me? I'm guessing it was Costin's idea since he so desperately wanted me marked, but I didn't want this coming from just anyone.

He looked offended. "You could do worse."

Of course, they all could read my mind. I really needed to figure out a way to level the playing field.

"No, I know. I don't mean it like that, but, well, I really hoped Nico would do it, I'm sorry." I didn't know what it all meant. If Nico didn't mark me, could he still turn me into a vampire? Nico couldn't want this vampire to mark me. If push came to shove, he would have to though. It would be to keep me safe, so it would be all I could do. Hopefully Nico would return from Paris with good news so Pablo and I wouldn't have to get to know each other too intimately.

"I understand. He should be back tonight, with luck," Pablo said, inching closer to me.

I stared out over the town, where statues were illuminated by street lights and water danced out of fountains. I was still keenly aware of the vampire that was moving next to me but I tried to ignore him. Pablo kept gravitating towards me until I was convinced that I was going to slide off the roof if he kept it up. I wasn't sure if I should move farther away and risk being rude, but he was beginning to encroach on my personal space.

I kept glancing at him from the corner of my eye and watched him move at an incredibly slow rate towards me. He was less than a few inches away when I finally scooted myself over one tile.

He seemed to catch on. "Forgive me, but I haven't fed in a few days. Would you allow me a…drink?"

"Go ahead," I said absently, still watching the fountains below.

He closed the distance between us instantly, his mouth open and fangs peering out from his upper lip.

My eyes widened. "Me?" My voice cracking with surprised horror.

He nodded his head once, leaning his mouth against my neck.

"Ummm…I…I would prefer not to." I inched a few tiles away. This was beyond awkward. No vampire had fed from me yet. It was going to be inevitable based on the company I was keeping, but there had to be some other mortal that he could drink from. Maybe I could even find someone for him to show how appreciative I was for him coming to my assistance. As long as it wasn't my neck that he used to drink from.

Pablo looked confused and backed away a little. "Do you not let Nico?"

I shook my head slowly and instinctively put my hand to my neck. "No, he has never asked." It made me stop to think. Should I have offered? Was it the thing to do in this kind of relationship? Nico has never said anything, or made a move to show he wanted to, so….

Pablo composed himself quickly and with a little embarrassment. "Yes, of course. Where are my manners?" He sat up straight and kept a safe distance between us. "It is just that your blood is right at the surface because of your nerves and it is making it difficult to concentrate. I would go hunt. However, I need to stay with you."

I nodded. "I'm sorry I've caused you so many problems." I didn't know what else to say. I knew my apology was lame, but maybe when Costin or Nico got here, then he could go hunting. As long as I didn't have to be a donor...

"It is not a problem. I was simply careless. Apologies." He moved a few tiles away from me, as though removing himself from the temptation.

Now what? I thought to myself, wondering if I was just supposed to sit on the roof until Nico came. It wasn't like I was just going to shimmy myself down the drain pipe and walk home, although I may have to at this point.

"So…." I said, casually after a few minutes of silence had passed between us.

He glanced at me. "Yes?"

"Is there anything I can do? I could go with you while you hunt."

He shook his head. "That's not necessary. I can wait. At least I understand why you reacted in the way you did."

"What do we do now?" I asked, wondering if there was some master plan or if he had some sort of telepathic line to Costin to know if I was going to be safe from Olivier for a while or when Nico would show up.

Pablo shrugged. "I do not know." He glanced up at the dark night for a moment as if looking for something. "For now, we wait."

"Great," I said half to myself as I shifted my weight slightly to get more comfortable. My stomach growled of hunger and I coughed a little to muffle the sound.

"You could tell me about Spain," I suggested, looking to fill the silence.

"What do you want to know?"

I shrugged. "Anything."

He began to talk to me about the tourist sites and some of his favorite places to go. After a while, the conversation faded. We had nothing else to say to each other.

The two of us sat in silence and watched Florence fall asleep. The crowds below dwindled down, walking into their homes and hotels. Stores closed, locked their doors, and turned their lights off. I let out a sigh and looked at Pablo who was a few feet away from me. He sat statuesque and stared into the night sky.

He finally turned to me and held out his hand and I glanced down at it. "You ready?"

"No Nico tonight?" I asked, though I already knew the answer. I was hesitant to take his hand as I didn't know what it all meant. Because Nico didn't show, did that mean I was being marked by Pablo?

"It appears not, but we need to get you home." Before I could ask, he answered my question. "I think it is safe to wait one more night before I handle marking you."

With his response, I accepted his outstretched hand and he gracefully plucked us from the rooftop to the side street below us.

"Can I trust you?" Pablo asked as we walked to my apartment.

I slowed my pace a little so I could look at him. "I think you can, yes, since I trusted you enough to save my life," I responded, waiting for what he was going to ask of me.

"I am going to need to sleep in your spare room so I can keep watch of you, but I need to make sure I am not disturbed. You must not enter the room so as not to let daylight in. Can you do this?"

I hesitated just a moment. "Yes, but - there is a window in the room. Daylight will come in through the blinds."

"There are shutters to make it light proof, I am sure. This is Nico's apartment, yes?" He asked, sounding very sure of himself.

I nodded. I guess Nico had taken precautions for himself I hadn't even been aware of. That means he could spend the night with me if he wanted, which he never had. Was it a trust issue or something else stopping him?

We entered the apartment and he quickly went towards the guest room. "Remember," he said closing the door. "This door must remain closed until I open it tonight."

I nodded. "I got it."

The apartment was quiet and the excitement from the past several hours swirled around me. Sleeping was the last thing on my mind. I didn't have to work. What was I supposed to do for the next twelve hours? My fingers danced around the spines of the books on the bookshelf. I reached for Shakespeare, hoping that it would be enough to put me to sleep within the next hour.

Before making myself comfortable in bed, I poured a glass of Chianti. Satisfied that alcohol and Shakespeare would do the trick, I climbed under the covers with only a hint of light coming from my nightstand.

Chapter 13

THE SUN HAD already set for the evening when I heard some noises from the spare bedroom. I turned off the television, making sure that the sounds did in fact come from where I thought they did. I padded down the hall to see if Pablo was okay. I didn't want to open the door as there was still a glimmer of light in the sky and I wasn't sure if it was enough to burn him.

"Pablo?" I whispered next to the door.

There was a low grumbling. "I am here," he replied. "Patience."

Hmm. Well I guess he's up and fine. Just as I was waiting for him to come out for the night, the front door opened.

"Dylan."

I turned around to find Nico. "You're back!"

"Yes, *mia mortale*," he said, kissing my forehead. He turned his attention to Pablo, who had exited from the guest room. "Thank you for assisting us. I hope we did not keep you from too much business in Barcelona."

"Not at all. It was my pleasure. You have quite a magnificent girl here, Nico." Pablo smiled at me. "Now, save us all and mark her."

Agitation filled his tone. As I watched him from the corner of my eye, I noticed how different he looked from the night before. His eyes were set deep in his head and his skin was paler. He looked almost ill. Was that from not feeding?

Nico pulled me into his embrace with a grin and then looked at Pablo. "Yes, I will take care of that."

"Great, I'll leave you be. I have some things I must do, as well. You may always call me if you are in need of assistance." Pablo jumped from the balcony and was gone before either of us could thank him.

"Are you alright?" Nico whispered into my ear.

I nodded, wrapping my arms around his neck. He held me close to his chest, leaving no room between us.

"It's okay." I could tell that Nico wanted to say something else but he remained silent.

I clung to his side, my heart beating faster with him next to me. "I was really worried about you."

"You needn't. I am strong, but did not like leaving you. I do appreciate you finding Costin to assist me."

"It was the least I could do. I knew as soon as I heard his voice that it would be trouble. I didn't think you two would actually get into a physical altercation, though. So much for being able to talk it out."

"Olivier is a very unreasonable being."

"He's different."

"How do you mean?"

I hesitated. "He has powers. Costin, Pablo, and I saw them."

Nico nodded. "His sovereign told me about them. They are not typically attributed to a vampire, but we do not know anything about who Olivier was prior to being made a vampire and that makes him more dangerous."

There was silence between us for a few moments. He didn't know what to say neither did I. We both knew that safety wasn't guaranteed until Olivier was under control. Nico was the only person I could count on to protect me, yet I needed to protect him as well. This new world I had been dragged into was much more dangerous than I had anticipated. Worrying kind of went with the territory all of a sudden. Nico was my only true protector in this new world I had been dragged into.

He quietly brought me into his arms and rocked me

like a child. Before I realized what was happening, the wall I had been trying to build around my fears came crashing down. I was crying hysterically into his chest and despite my tries, I couldn't calm myself.

"Dylan, Dylan, it's okay, I'm here now."

"I know, it's just…Olivier and then…Pablo…." I choked out between sobs.

"Shhh," he cooed. "Tell me what happened."

I let my mind race with everything that had happened in the past day. It was too much to deal with and I kept crying until there were no more tears left.

"Pablo tried to feed from you?" His voice raised an extra octave.

I nodded. "He was nice enough about it when he realized he had scared me, but yes."

Nico shook his head. "O positive. It's his weakness…I should have known. I'm sorry."

"Huh?" I looked at him, completely bewildered.

"Your blood type is O positive. Blood types for us are like," he thought for a moment, "like different kinds of wines, if you will. We all have our favorites."

My eyes widened. This wasn't something I could deal with right now. My mind was already on overload. I glanced away fast so Nico wouldn't see the horror that must have flashed through my eyes. Did Nico not like O positive, which made it easier to be around me? What blood types *did* he like?

Nico was apologizing incessantly, so I tried to change the subject a little. "Did you find Olivier's sovereign?"

"Yes, and Henri has apologized. Olivier is a constant problem for him in Paris. Apparently Olivier has a few tricks up his sleeves and no one has been able to figure out why or how he has them."

"Yes, we got to see some of that first hand."

"He's taking care of the problem as we speak."

My eyebrows rose. "Oh?" I wanted to ask how, though I wasn't sure if I wanted to know the answer. As long as he was being taken care of, that was good enough for me.

"Do not worry about these things. Everything will be fine now."

"Can you mark me now?" I asked, pressing myself closer to him. I felt like I was asking for something indecent, something sinful. I'd had enough excitement over the past couple days and wanted this mark more than I would have ever thought possible.

Nico closed the gap between our mouths. His lips were cold on mine and I had forgotten how much I missed the sensation. "With pleasure."

"Now?" I asked, pulling away a little.

"*Mia mortale*, you just asked me to mark you, no?" He backed up from me to read my full facial expressions.

"Yes, but, so eagerly?" I knew it was foolish, but it wasn't something that should just be rushed into. Now that the danger was gone, I could be a little particular, right?

"Whenever you are ready, Dylan." Nico curled up on the couch with me in his arms.

I opened my mouth to say something but quickly closed it. With all that had taken place in the past 24 hours, I wanted to be selfish and just curl up with Nico for a little while. While I had so many questions still to ask, I didn't want to ask them any longer. I feared I would get the answers much sooner than the year I was originally told of.

Nico kissed my forehead as we continued to get comfortable, as if pushing my worries away. How often did he listen to my thoughts? My mind was probably an open book for him, so what did he think of the reading material?

Chapter 14

WE HAD TO wait until the next night because of the nearing daylight for the mark to be made. Last night, Nico stayed with me until the last possible moment for both of our sakes. The later he stayed, the less chance Olivier would still be out. He had refused to stay in the guest room and instead chose to go to his place. Regardless, I had fallen asleep in his arms and dreamed of how I was to be marked. I woke alone.

Nico had just stepped out of the shower and steam poured out of the bathroom. He was convinced that taking a hot shower would warm him up enough to make it more pleasurable for me. I wasn't going to argue as long as I got to enjoy his body again, hot or cold.

"How should we do this?"

A towel wrapped low on his body barely covered

what it was supposed to and left his groin just visible at the top. Droplets of water clung to his chest like morning dew on a leaf. His hair was spiked in a thousand different directions from the moisture, too.

"There's different ways?" I asked, not sure what he meant. I couldn't think straight with his body just a cloth away from being completely nude. I lay back on the bed and waited for him to make his move. I was hoping he'd just jump on the bed and ravage me because that was all I could think about.

"This is new to me, as well," he smiled. He rubbed his hands in his hair while giving me a look that melted me to the core.

"We could...." I let the thought trail off.

"Yes?" He asked eagerly, as if he knew exactly what I was going to suggest.

"Make love." It was a simple request, though I felt dirty asking for it. I was never in complete control of myself with him this close, I couldn't think of anything else. Being near him was unlike any other experience for me. Sure there'd been other men, but Nico was different. He was intoxicating and an addiction was quickly forming.

"Excuse me?" A grin was tugging at the corner of his mouth and he fought hard not to let it spread.

"You heard me."

I wanted him and the anticipation was building beyond my control. I knew the mark would hurt because he had warned me of it multiple times. I was ready for it, though, because the pleasure would outrank the pain, or at least that's what I was counting on.

"Dylan, I left bruises the last time we…."

"And I told you I didn't mind." It was true, though. I had bruised in bright purplish-blue splotches along my inner thighs and around my shoulders where he had held me. The sheer strength of him left marks on my human skin, yet it had felt so good as it happened that I didn't complain. His body didn't give like mine and it was like pushing on a wall—no matter how much you pushed, the wall stood still. Making love to something that powerful was exhilarating and the souvenir marks were just a small price to pay.

His face showed some hesitance. I knew he didn't want to hurt me, though I was counting on the notion that he wanted me just as much as I wanted him. A few bruises shouldn't stop him, though I could imagine what it looked like.

I let out a soft sigh. "Please don't make me ask again."

"You're impossible." His tone was of disapproval, though his face said otherwise.

"Would you really have it any other way?"

"Vieni qui, mia mortale."

I went to him eager and wet. It had been almost a week since the first time we had made love and I was ready for round two, especially since the bruises had healed.

His towel dropped at the foot of the bed and I took in every line of his body. His pale arms pressed into the comforter and I watched how the muscles in his arms tensed. I watched for the rise and fall of his chest but there wasn't any.

"You're not breathing," I gasped. His glistening pectorals hovered above me, statuesque. His chest was completely and utterly still.

"Sometimes I forget to when I'm in highly emotional states." He climbed onto the bed and inched closer to me. "Like now."

I parted my legs, inviting him up the length of me. The corners of his mouth twitched into a smirk as he made his way up my body.

He laughed as he watched my face process the new information. "Why does it surprise you?"

"I guess nothing should by now," I giggled.

Every two or three inches, he stopped to brush his lips against my skin. My hands played in the short curls of his hair, which was still wet from the shower. I let out a soft moan as he kissed my navel.

I felt his lips stop. "Dylan?"

"Don't stop," I found myself pleading. I knew he was questioning whether the sound was one of pain or pleasure. This time it was of the latter and I couldn't bear the pause in our activities, no matter how brief.

"I'm trying to go slow and carefully is all," he admitted.

"Don't…just…."

He continued to slide his lips against me and up the length of my torso. When he reached my neck, he slowly made his way back down. He moved the fabric of my panties down to kiss the side of my hip.

My body quivered unexpectedly, and my spine bowed, bidding him nearer.

"Mmmm, that was nice," he murmured against my navel. "Do it again."

I laughed softly. His hands were moving up my thighs, circling more intimately to the ultimate place of desire. The coldness of his fingertips left goose bumps as he continued exploring. He was driving me slowly mad, toying with my warm-blooded cravings. His fingers looped over the elastic of my panties and tugged gently. I let him slide them down my legs, only to be tossed off the edge of the bed.

His right hand cupped the side of my hip while his left hand roamed lower and sent me closer to the brink of pleasure. I writhed in ecstasy and my hips rose off the mattress.

"I will be as careful as I can," he warned against my ear.

I nodded. As my hips squirmed upward to meet him, Nico met me with his own excitement and pounded me back down flat against the bed. Over and over he drove into me while his own cries of passion escaping his lips. I raised my mouth to his to swallow some of the sound. I kissed him as if I was drinking him and consuming him in order to gain more pleasure.

"Careful," he warned as my tongue traced along one of his incisors. His mouth moved down my neck, across my throat. I could feel my breath catch a little as he licked the skin which lay across my heavily pulsating jugular. I could see the grin on his face as my breathing got shorter and more labored. He moved back up the length of me, stroking my hair back from my face.

I wrapped my arms around his neck, coaching him further and deeper. He stared into my eyes, hypnotizing me with pools of sapphire blue. He stayed focused on me as he kept pushing me further over the edge. I could feel a smile spreading on his face as he gave me what I wanted and reveled in the pleasure. It was more than simple delight – it was maddening waves of bliss. I was surprised to find my body felt no pain from the hard flesh that rhythmically drove into me.

We fell into a crumpled, sweaty heap on the bed. I curled into the side of him, tired and suddenly sore. Truthfully, I was in agony, as though my entire body had been in a fight I wasn't a part of. It was a pain I didn't mind dealing with as the final waves continued to pulse through me, though another part of me argued otherwise.

"I didn't even feel the mark," I commented, letting my fingers trace down his chest.

There was silence on the other side of the bed. I waved my hand in front of his face and concentrated on him.

"Nico?"

He let out an exasperated sigh. "It isn't my fault. You distracted me."

"You didn't mark me?"

"Dylan, when I mark you, you'll know it. For one, you'll be bleeding and secondly, I am sure you will be in an extreme amount of discomfort."

I was sore now, so I didn't know what he was holding back for. There must have been something in my face that made him suddenly concerned.

"I hurt you, didn't I?"

"The good kind, I promise," I answered with a bright grin. I wanted to sound as convincing as possible because I truly enjoyed myself too much during to give him a reason to stop.

"Dylan, we can't keep doing this. I am trying to hold back and be careful, but it is so difficult. You give yourself so freely that I simply cannot focus on anything but the pleasure."

My cheeks burned crimson as I listened to him talk. "Sorry," I apologized. "I just can't help myself."

"Neither can I," he pulled me closer. "Why didn't you tell me I was hurting you?"

"There wasn't any pain *during* it."

"Perhaps I shouldn't shield you so much then," he figured, more to himself than to me.

My eyebrows rose. "How do you mean?"

He wore a pained expression and it was obvious he did not want to explain himself. "It isn't mind control," he said quickly. "Well, perhaps it is, to an extent, but I'm able to absorb some of the pain you feel. It is something I was doing without really thinking about it."

"Oh." What the hell was I supposed to say to that?

If I was still experiencing the pain while he was shielding, I was glad to know I hadn't felt the full extent. If it had been too much more, it would have outweighed the waves of pleasure. If only the aftermath could be shielded as well – I knew I'd have a new set of bruises, but I didn't mind.

Making love to him was like making love to a God, and the marks were just something that came with the territory. The levels of ecstasy were too high to deny just because of some pain.

"You're not upset?"

"No, I'm relieved you've been doing it."

He shook his head and made a face at my naivety. "You don't mind I've been using mind control on you just so we can…"

"No," I interrupted. I leaned in to kiss him on the lips before continuing, "I don't mind. What's the alternative? Wait a year to continue this? I'm not willing to wait, unless you're saying you are?"

He shook his head. "I suppose not, though I worry I'm doing more harm than good."

"Don't be ridiculous. The bruises heal. It's not like I've got broken bones or anything." I stared into his face and while he seemed satisfied with what I was saying, there was still something on his mind. "What now?" I asked while adjusting the sheets across me.

"We still have the concern of the mark."

"Yes, we do," I agreed. I had almost forgotten about it until he brought it up.

A brief knock and the sound of the apartment door opening brought us both back to reality. I grabbed wads of sheets to cover myself as Nico jumped off the bed in an attempt to throw some clothes on.

Costin turned the corner into our bedroom. I was wondering why we even bothered with a front door if he was going to walk in whenever he pleased.

"Sorry to interrupt," Costin greeted us as his eyes took in the scene. I could only imagine what he thought of the two of us by now.

I held the sheets in front of me, sitting up in the bed. "Hi." I knew my face was bright red as there was no hiding what had just transpired. Costin's mouth twitched in a grin as he looked at us.

"Marking?" he asked, looking at Nico.

I looked away, not wanting to be the one to break the news. The room smelled like sex and I wished we could have been given some kind of notice we were going to have company. Nico could read minds, so wasn't he able to tell when Costin was coming?

"What brings you over?" Nico asked, trying for a nonchalant subject change while buttoning his shirt. He exited the room with Costin and allowed me a chance to get dressed.

"Damn it," I heard Costin say. I knew he was scolding Nico for not marking me. I wondered if Nico was telling him exactly why that was, though I figured Costin was pretty well clued in. "The two of you have to stop being so reckless. You know you could seriously injure her, right? I mean, either through the act or by not marking her, you're taking chances."

"I know, I know. But can we focus? What's going on?" Nico asked, trying to get Costin to the point of his visit.

"We have some problems. Henri will be joining us in a few minutes to discuss everything, but Olivier is stronger than any of us anticipated. For someone who has only twenty years, he is a force to be reckoned with." Costin spoke loud enough that I could hear as I frantically looked for my shirt in the pile of discarded clothes on the floor.

"What does that mean exactly?" I asked after I stepped out of the room. I had a few ideas running around in my head, though none of the conclusions sounded very positive.

Nico was leaning against the back of the couch, his arms crossed over his chest. I could tell he didn't like Costin barging in on us, especially with bad news. I walked over and stood beside him.

Costin glanced over at me. "It means Henri isn't able to handle him. Olivier is quite powerful and does not follow the rules as he should."

I looked at the two of them as if they were speaking their own language.

"If Olivier battles Henri and wins, he will become the new sovereign," Costin explained. "Olivier will rule Paris and it's likely that he will he not follow rules and he won't expect any of his subjects to, either."

"We can't let that happen, obviously," Nico interjected. "So what do we need to do?"

Costin shook his head. "I don't know. Let's just wait until Henri arrives."

"When can we expect him?" I asked. I had looked up at the clock and realized it was already two in the morning.

"Soon," Costin said, looking at his watch.

"You are welcome to go to bed mia mortale," Nico said. "I know you must be tired."

Costin let out a chuckle and disguised it with a cough. My cheeks burned with embarrassment, but I shook my head. "It's okay. I want to meet Henri, too."

We simply stood there in awkward silence.

The living room was completely silent, except for my own breathing. I was the only one alive in the room, I noted with some amusement. The large moon outside the largest of the windows was providing enough light for tonight. Plus, Costin insisted on natural lighting whenever possible since fluorescent lights gave him a headache. The icemaker dumped some cubes automatically and the introduction of a new sound made me jump.

Costin and Nico stood across from each other like statues as I paced from room to room. I was trying to take my mind off the idea of yet another vampire was going to be coming over. I was comfortable with Nico, that was a given. Costin had proven himself to be on our side and he was Nico's sovereign, but a new guy *and* one who oversaw Olivier? I just wasn't able to calm my nerves, so I moved magazines from one table to another, made my bed, straightened picture frames, anything I could think of.

I made my way into the living room, fluffing the cushions on the couch when Nico reached out and grabbed my wrist. I paused and looked up into his eyes, pleading to let me go.

"Stop," he whispered, releasing me.

I let the cushion drop from my hand and walked into the kitchen. I opened a bottle of wine and fought the urge to drink right from the bottle. It was certainly one way of handling the situation. I could just get drunk and pretend it was all a bad hallucination. I looked over at the men and they just stood there calmly and quietly. It was unnerving to watch them and their lack of movement.

"He's here," Costin finally said as he took a step towards the front door.

Our awaited visitor, Henri, strode in with his feet barely touching the ground. He wore a long leather jacket swaying back and forth in an invisible breeze as he stepped. The high collar stood away from his neck and he let his long brown hair flow loosely down his back. His skin was milky white, much paler than any of the others. He definitely didn't start his life with an olive tone like the Italian men to my right. Dark blue eyes pierced my concentration as he walked past me and extended a hand to Costin.

Is being absolutely gorgeous some sort of prerequisite to being a vampire around here?

"Mia mortale," Nico interrupted my daydream. "Please keep in mind we can all read your thoughts," he added with some agitation. The jealousy was clear in his tone as well as his actions, as he moved in closer to my side and reminding me who I was supposed to be captivated by. Costin choked out a laugh but quickly put his hand to his mouth as though he was coughing.

"Of course," I whispered. Had Nico been jealous of my thoughts? Had Henri really heard me? As I glanced sideways at him, I doubted it. If he had, he showed no emotion towards my straying thoughts.

"Have the two of you met?" Costin questioned Nico and Henri, taking the heat off me. I thanked him silently in my head.

Henri flashed a grin at Nico. "Yes, though it's been at least a century. I almost didn't recognize you with the short hair."

Nico instinctively ran his fingers through the short curls. "Just trying to keep up with the times."

I was staring at Nico and trying to picture him with longer hair. I couldn't conjure an image and wasn't sure I wanted to. I liked running my hands through his short curls. He had never mentioned anything about it, though it's not like it would have come up in conversation, either.

"Yes, Dylan," he announced. "I had hair longer than Costin's when I was first turned. Over the centuries I have shortened it, as it became more fashionable for men to have shorter hair."

"Huh," I said as casually as I could muster.

I looked slowly between the men and they all seemed to be waiting for some additional comments or questions from me. When I chose not to say anything, they continued on about their conversation.

This was a good opportunity to go in the kitchen and pour another glass. Since they didn't seem to be slowing down in their conversations, I might as well go ahead and work through a bottle of Chianti. Maybe the alcohol would even make it easier to listen to the vampire politics a little bit more.

Part of me was wishing I was at the bar, flipping bottles and pouring shots instead of standing here, but Nico smiled over at me when I had the wine glass to my lips. How could I not appreciate this man? With the glass in hand, I sat down on the couch in front of the men to learn about everything that had and has yet to take place.

Henri turned his attention on me suddenly, watching me without any thought of hiding his peaked interest in me. He stared at me as though he had just noticed I was in the room, as if I had been invisible until I had uttered the last comment. Minutes passed as he continued his inventory and I wondered what the others were thinking about his open display of voyeurism.

"So you're Dylan," he finally stated.

I nodded, not knowing what to say. It was one of those obvious statements since I was the only mortal in the room. Who else would I be? I kept my thoughts in check so I did not insult him.

He seemed to be smelling something in the air, his nostrils flaring. I sniffed, too, not smelling anything pungent. I was trying to follow the scent without attracting everyone's attention. The only thing I had cooked here was a few days ago and I knew I kept a clean house.

"O positive," he said with a grin.

Nico and Costin nodded in unison, confirming Henri's comment.

"Ah, yes. That seems to be biting me in the ass

frequently," I said, trying to lighten the mood.

Henri chuckled and turned to Nico. "Real live one you have."

"That I do."

"Where is Olivier now?" Costin asked, getting back on track.

"He is back in Paris. He will not apologize and he believes he is still in the right for coming after Dylan," Henri explained. "I cannot guarantee that he will stay there."

"And why not? You are his sovereign, are you not?" Nico demanded.

Costin put his hand out. "I apologize for his bluntness, but I must ask the same."

"You already know that Olivier is not your ordinary vampire. He was only made into one a few years ago, yet he has the power of one who is centuries old."

"So I've been told," Costin said.

"Is there anything we can do?" I asked. All three glanced at me, as though I had spoken out of turn. My heart skipped a beat and I took a step closer to the couch. My natural instinct was to run out of the room, but I kept my feet planted and desperately fought the urge to flee.

"It is the only thing I can offer right now. I would suggest your...," he hesitated, and we all knew what he wanted to say. Lover. It reverberated inside my head and I waited for him to say it. "I suggest that Nico mark you sooner than later. Pablo or Costin can, too, but it is not safe for you to remain unmarked and human as long as Olivier exists. I cannot rightfully condemn him to death when he currently has equal rights to you, even if I agree with your situation."

"Equal rights?" Nico asked. "How do you figure?"

Henri made a gesture with his hands. "He saw her in Paris. It was his move to make and he thought he had more time to play a game of cat and mouse as he hadn't expected her to run into another one of us."

"That's bullshit and you know it," Nico said. "He had the chance to do something and then she came to Italy. It was our turn to take care of the problem."

I wanted to speak up and say something but I kept quiet. As Costin had once mentioned, my scent was all over Nico, and the other way around. Just because I didn't have some stupid mark wasn't enough to give Olivier the right to abduct me.

I didn't expect Henri to care about me, but I would have liked him to at least take care of Olivier. I felt as if Olivier should have been punished, or killed, or...I don't know. Just being kept in Paris wasn't enough.

"Is that how you see it? I don't. We both knew she was human and had to deal with her. You and Olivier both seem to fancy the girl, yet neither of you did as you should have and just marked her. Or killed her and been done with the whole damn thing."

Something told me that if it were Henri that had seen me first, I wouldn't be sitting here. He would have "taken care of the problem" without hesitating. Now Olivier didn't seem so bad in comparison to what I could have encountered in Paris.

If the situation presented itself, I didn't believe Henri would defend us. He would not come to aid Nico and Costin to protect me. Instead, he would allow Olivier to get to me. I wanted to ask or hear the question asked, but Henri was intimidating. As I stood there, I saw his jaw set firmly. He waited for someone to respond to him or dismiss him. He seemed to think we were wasting his time and I knew he wanted to be in Paris more than here right now. I was content with him going back to France. He made me very uncomfortable.

"I will mark her tonight," Nico stated as he pulled me towards him. I clung to him and didn't argue as I tried to determine how long Olivier would stay in Paris for.

Costin glanced at us curiously. "No excuses, Nico." There was some question to his voice, as though he didn't trust either of us to make sure it was done. "You'll mark her? Tonight?"

Nico nodded in silence.

"I will let Pablo know he can return to Spain," Costin remarked with a grin. "It's unfortunate, though. He was really looking to help out."

"Yeah, by helping out, you mean helping himself to some O positive," Nico tossed back.

O positive was the most common blood type in the United States, however over here, the derivatives of A were more common.

"I've never been a big fan of it, myself," Costin said and winked at me. "It doesn't have enough flavor."

Nico nodded. "I wouldn't say no flavor, it is certainly better than A. Now B positive on the other hand…"

"Ahh yes, B positive. I was able to enjoy that almost nightly when I was in Asia back in the 1800s. I had to force myself to leave because I thought I'd bleed the entire population." He laughed

Henri chimed in, "Any of the positives will work for me, though I like B the best as well. I would rather starve myself before I go for O negative." They all agreed and chuckled.

I knew they were talking about this in front of me to tease me, but the conversation still didn't sit well with me. I guess I should be happy to have the blood type I did, considering the company I kept. "I guess it means not too many American tourists turn up missing, huh?"

The vampires began to laugh.

"That is true. I suppose the US embassy should thank us," Henri added.

Chapter 15

A KNOCK ON my apartment door startled me. Nico normally just walked in, though maybe he was being formal since I was supposed to be marked tonight.

I peeked out the blinds and noted that it was still daylight. My dozing on the couch made me lose track of the time. My habits were slowly turning nocturnal, but the sun was still welcome in my life, even though I didn't see it nearly as often as in the past. I hadn't been expecting anyone – at least not anyone who would be knocking during the day. I laughed; this was the life I was leading.

There was no peep hole on the door and no windows that overlooked the door. I would have to talk to Nico about that to see what he could do. I didn't do well with strangers, especially since he could never be with me during the day.

Another knock sounded, this time louder and more impatient. I hesitated and debated if I should pretend no one was home. Whoever was knocking would get the hint and go away. The knocking persisted and curiosity got the best of me since whoever was on the other side of the door was determined to get the door to open.

I finally undid the deadbolt and opened the door, slow and cautious. A smiling blonde beamed at me as I peeked out over the chain that kept the door from swinging wide open. I swallowed hard in dread of the figure in front of me.

"Dylan!" She shrieked.

I moved the chain and she pushed the door open all the way, pulling me into her embrace.

"Jen – hi!" I greeted. Jen was supposed to be in Florida where I left her. I knew why she was here. I hadn't called her in a while partly because Costin confiscated my phone like a child out of fear that I'd make contact with her. Ha. Little did he know Jen. Figures she'd manage a way out here, even if it did mean getting on a plane. For as long as I've known her, she's never done that.

But how did she find me? She only knew the hotel I was staying at, not Nico's apartment. She kept her arms wrapped in a tight hold across my chest until I thought I was going to suffocate.

"You can release me now," I gasped.

She did as I asked and gave me a push in the chest. "I should give you a good bitch slap is what I should do."

I laughed and took a step back. I wouldn't put it past her to actually do it. If it were the other way around, I'd probably do the same thing.

Jen had gotten a call right before meeting Nico. Once I met him, I forgot about her. She passed through my mind once after the mind blowing sex with Nico because I wanted to tell her about it. That's when Costin took my phone.

She was from my *other* life, the one I chose to give up when I became part of Nico's. She was also the sister of Chris. He broke my heart and she was there to help pick up the pieces that her brother had smashed. She kept smiling at me and I forced my "happy to see you" face on.

Having her here brought my two worlds crashing together and I wasn't sure if I could handle that. I held the door open and stood there dumbfounded. I didn't know what to say or do with her, for that matter.

"Nice place," she said as she pushed past me and walked into the living room. She dropped a suitcase I hadn't initially seen next to the door. "So now I know you're still alive, which room is mine?"

"How did you find me?" I knew that I sounded rude. There would be no other reason she came to Italy besides to see me - and here I was asking how she found me.

"It took a while since you didn't leave a forwarding address at your hotel," she boasted her detective skills. "You sound like you didn't want to be found."

She was right. Jen was my best friend because she could read me better than anyone else in the world. Hell, she understood me better than I did sometimes. I could never figure out how she could do that when her brother couldn't. Chris could never read what was on my mind or what I wanted.

Now Jen was here. I wanted to leave my old life behind me and now she was *here* and posed a reminder of friends and obligations. The flip side was she was a close friend and I finally had someone human to hang around with while the sun was still out.

Human. That sent a sudden trigger through my head. It was approaching dusk and Nico would be here soon to mark me. Jen couldn't have picked a worse time to come, but there was a part of me that was glad she was here. With Olivier in Paris, I was out of harm's way. I needed something to take my mind off this crazy new life I had been pushed in to. Since it happened, I've been swept up in a whirlwind of events without any time to digest everything. Jen could be the mortal distraction that I needed. She could also help me remember why I left Florida to make this whole immortality thing seem like the best idea ever.

"I'm glad you're here, Jen," I finally said, closing the door.

She looked around and ran her fingers along the cushions of the couch and around the carved wooden tables. "How can you afford this place? You've been gone for over a month and have to be out of money by now, right?"

I changed the subject since I did not know how to answer her questions. "So how *did* you find me?"

"When I asked about you at the hotel you told me about, the front desk clerk told me you had checked out a few days ago."

I remembered telling her about the hotel since it had been the only way I could get her off the phone. Now I regretted it. I looked over at Jen to find her face was painted with exhaustion and I knew she hadn't even checked into a hotel. She still had the look of being on an airplane for the long flight and she smelled of sweat.

"Mmm hmm," I urged her to continue.

"Well, then the bell hop interrupted and told me he hailed a taxi for you a few days ago to take you here." She smiled at me. "It's really good to see you. You look great, even if you are a little pale."

I returned the gesture yet stayed silent. Stupid bell hop. I didn't know what to say to her. I have to guard everything I say since she was part of my old life and definitely didn't fit into the new one. What would Nico say about my visitor? She was going to start asking questions that I could not answer, at least not honestly. I could feel it by the way she studied the apartment. There was nothing I could tell her about my new life. I couldn't risk introducing her to Nico and I certainly couldn't risk her meeting Olivier if he chose to come back. So now what? I would only be able to dodge her questions for so long before she got nosy and tried her detective skills again without my consent. Who knows what she'd be able to find out.

"This place is really nice. It looks expensive!" She flopped down on the couch and kicked off her shoes. "I'm beat."

I walked into the kitchen to avoid any immediate questions. Maybe she'd just take a nap for a few hours. "Do you want some water or anything?"

"Sure." I could see her eyes getting heavy as she sat with her feet stretched out on the arm of the couch. All of the makeup she was so accustomed to wearing had worn off during the flight and the running around. She wasn't the model of perfection as I always thought of her. It was all foundation and blush, which somehow made me feel better about my own image.

I walked out of the kitchen with a bottle of sparkling

water. I set it on the table in front of her and took a seat in the chair across the room.

"Sparkling?" she asked, picking up the bottle.

Once upon a time, I could never drink sparkling, though it seemed that was all that was around. I had always thought it was more bubbles than water, like non-alcoholic champagne or something. The Italians refer to the water as either "gas or no gas" to the tourists, which still amuses me. I nodded. "It takes getting used to, though the regular stuff is just horrible."

She shrugged and took a few sips. Her head lolled to the side and she yawned. Her hand went quickly to her mouth to mask the signs of being tired, but I saw it. She was never one to admit being tired. Instead, she was the epitome of the party girl.

I pointed towards the room down the hall. "I have a guest room – why don't you take a nap? You've got to be exhausted."

Jen looked over at me, a little embarrassed I caught her falling asleep. "Do you mind? I feel bad, though, I just found you."

"Don't worry about it. I've got to do some shopping anyways – I've hardly got any groceries in the house. Rest up so we can go out tonight."

That caught her attention. "Out? Like out on the

town?"

"Only if you want to," I coaxed, knowing that she wouldn't be able to resist.

"You know me too well, Dylan," she replied as she swung her feet off the couch. She got up and dragged her suitcase down the hall.

I listened to her unzip her luggage and then the squeak of the mattress. She'd be out in minutes. I closed my eyes and leaned into the cushion of the chair a little. How was I going to get out of this one?

It was nice to be awake during the daylight hours for a change. The supermarket nearest me closed at dusk, so I almost never made it over there in time to get groceries and my kitchen cabinets were severely suffering. I grabbed my purse and the apartment key and left Jen to sleep.

I walked back in with an armload of grocery bags and heard the shower running. *That was a quick nap.* I dumped the groceries across the kitchen counter, glad to be rid of the weight in my arms. I had picked up cereal, fruit, snacks, some deli meat, and bread. *Real food.* When I was with Nico, we'd typically stop into a wine bar and I'd get some sort of little aperitif, but I felt like I was always in a constant state of being hungry. My stomach hadn't completely adjusted to my new schedule.

I sat on the couch and settled in with my feet tucked up under me. I turned on the radio and grabbed a book I picked up at the market.

The door to the bathroom opened like a sauna with hot steam pouring out. Jen stepped out with hair piled into a towel on the top of her head and otherwise she was back to her regular self. Makeup was perfectly applied and her fitted jeans sat low on her slim hips.

"So," she said, sitting next to me on the couch, taking the book out of my hands.

"Yes?" I prepared myself for the worst. As I looked over at her, I thought she was going to explode with excitement.

"Have you met any hot Italian guys?" She asked, gushing and moving closer to me on the couch.

"A few," I managed. There, it was honest. I didn't have to give her all the details, but maybe I would be able to tell her enough to satisfy her curiosity without actually lying to her.

"Does this place belong to you or a guy?" Her eyes wandered across the expensive furniture spanning the two-bedroom flat. "I mean, unless you got a job here, there's no way you can afford this place. It's gotta cost at least seven hundred Euros a week, right?"

She was starting to ask questions that I was going to

have to answer with at least some honesty. In reality, I had no idea how much this place was, but Nico had taken care of all of it – and I was so appreciative that he had been so generous.

"Well, I did get a job," I remarked. "I'm a bartender."

She looked shocked. "What?"

I nodded. "As for the apartment, it belongs to a friend of mine." I hesitated with how much to tell her. She'd wonder if I was living with this 'friend' or if they had an extra place. I could get out of it easily enough by saying it was their rental property because, technically, Nico didn't live here with me. That would take the guesswork out of the equation when she saw that he didn't spend the night with me.

Her eyebrows raised in anticipation of some juicy gossip to chew on.

"Maybe he's a little more than a friend," I added.

"Now that's what I'm talking about," she giggled.

"What about you? How did you afford airfare to Florence?"

She went quiet and fidgeted with a tendril of hair that had fallen from the towel. It's been a bad habit of hers for as long as I've known her. "Promise not to lose it?"

Whenever Jen played with her hair nothing good ever came afterwards. "No promises," I said, turning my full attention to her. I almost didn't want to hear what her answer was but I knew I'd be mad, especially with a warning like that.

"You have to promise. It's the only way I'm telling." She stood there like a child, plea bargaining to make sure that she and I stayed on steady ground.

"Fine," I sighed. "I promise." I'd say whatever to get her to fess up at this point.

She bit the bottom of her lip and perused my face as she decided on how she was going to tell me. "Chris paid for my plane ticket. He was worried since you were supposed to be back over a week ago. No one's gotten a postcard from you in over two weeks and your hotel said you checked out." She took a few steps towards me as she said this, worried, I think, that I was going to break down. She was almost right.

"Chris?" I bit back. "Are you kidding me?" While I was glad Jen cared about me enough to get on a plane, I couldn't believe he shelled out the money to send her all the way over to Italy to check on me. He left me at the altar for God's sake. Why would he even care?

"You promised not to lose it," she whined.

"Damn it, Jen. I don't need you checking up on me so you can report back to your brother of all people. Tell him I'm fine and go." I stood up from the couch and paced back and forth.

She stood up and chased after me. She pinned me against the wall and placed her arm around me. "Dylan, come on! I'll only stay a little while, but can't we have some fun? I'll only tell him you're okay and I won't give him any details. Whatever you tell me to tell him is what I'll say. Okay?"

I didn't really have a choice. She was going to have to go back soon anyways and I wouldn't be able to stop her from telling Chris whatever she wanted to disclose. The important thing was to make sure she didn't learn too much, which was for her benefit, too.

"Fine, you can stay." I smiled, but anyone who knew me would see it was forced.

"Gee thanks."

I shook my head. "I'm sorry. I'm glad that you're here."

This was going to get awkward. I couldn't tell her the truth - that much I realized. What story was I going to give her? More importantly, how was I going to introduce her to Nico? Would she sense what he was or would she be like the thousands of others in the clubs and restaurants who never batted an eye? I was praying he'd eavesdrop tonight before barging in so he could prepare himself.

We talked through most of the afternoon and into the early evening of what was going on in Florida and the restaurant and her new job. I kept things focused on her and my old life, but mainly her.

"There is probably something else I should tell you,"

she said, suddenly quieter.

"Okay, what is it?" I asked, wondering what could make her go this silent so fast for the second time tonight.

She bit her lip unconsciously. "It's about Chris."

I wanted to tell her I didn't care. Most of me didn't actually care what happened to him, but that small part won over, especially since he was obviously curious about me. "What about him?" I tried not to sound overly interested.

"He's engaged."

I stared at her in disbelief. It had been only a little over six months since the wedding had been called off and last I knew, he wasn't even dating anyone. "Oh..."

"I know it's fast. That's what I told him, but he didn't seem to care what I thought," Jen said. "You know who she is, though."

It caught my attention. "I do?" I was racking my brain, trying to think of who I knew that would possibly want anything to do with Chris. All of my friends heard the stories of Chris and none of them seemed keen on how he had treated me. No one left their fiancée at the altar in front of all their friends, especially with no reason.

"You remember Amy, don't you?"

Amy was an assistant manager at the restaurant I worked at for a while, though she quit about a year ago to attend culinary school. Chefs, last I checked, were very career-focused, which was the very thing Chris used as an excuse to call off the wedding. That is, unless there was another reason he hadn't told me. Not giving me all the details would be very much like him. He was always omitting key information so he could still be liked. Whenever there was a situation that would put him at odds with someone, he left out anything that might get him in trouble. If Amy was a chef, then Chris hadn't left me for being obsessed with my job.

"Really? What is she doing these days?" I asked casually, trying not to look at her while I waited for her answer.

"She's a sous chef at the new hotel that opened up. Remember how she was going to culinary school?"

I nodded. All I could think about was how Chris was a lying bastard and I'd never learn the real reason why he never showed at the church. If I were in Florida I would have marched up to him and demanded answers. I could question Jen, but I didn't want her to know that I care about him. I don't, really. I'm over him, but I wish he had at least been honest with me. *Lying bastard.* I didn't want to talk about Chris any more. He was an old chapter. I had Nico now, who was like the Anti-Chris. That was one of the reasons he was so attractive to me.

"Good for him," I forced out to put an end to the

conversation.

"I'll let him know. I think that's why he sent me over here. He wanted to make sure you were okay with it. Maybe he doesn't want you causing problems at the wedding."

They didn't talk that often, so she was as clueless about him as I was.

As the sun set, I couldn't help but steal several glances at the clock. I wondered when Nico would make his appearance or if he was going to at all. The mark was supposed to be tonight and I desperately wanted to delay it now that Jen was here. Costin had said no more excuses, especially when Olivier was still out there. Sure, he was behaving himself for now, but as long as I was human and he was thirsty, I was never going to be completely at ease.

"Are you hungry?" I asked, finally, realizing it was eight o'clock. I knew the streets were getting crowded because I could hear the traffic getting heavier and the distant laughing of tourists out for the night.

"Starving! What's good around here?"

I grinned. "Everything! The food here is amazing. I did promise you a night out, unless you wanted to eat in. It's your choice." I knew which she'd pick but it was fun to play with her.

"Let's go out!" She smiled devilishly and I knew she wanted to check out the nightlife. Hopefully I could use this to get my mind off some things. The evening was relatively early, so there was time for marking later – much later.

As we stepped into our high heels, I knew we would have fun tonight. We headed out the door and down the street for cocktails to kick the evening into high gear. There were just some things you couldn't do in the company of vampires.

We went into a crowded bar and found a tall table to stand at. A waiter came over and we placed a drink order.

"I need to use the bathroom," Jen bellowed over the music. "Wait here."

I nodded to her and stood at the table, waiting for our drinks.

Nico appeared at my table instantly, like I had blinked him into existence.

"Hi," I greeted him.

"Get rid of her," he stated in a tone laced with irritation. When he didn't even give me a proper welcome, something was up.

"Nice to see you, too." I looked up at him, trying to figure out what was going on. "What's wrong?"

He stood there, giving nothing. "You need to get rid of her. Tonight."

I shook my head. "We need a plan B. She showed up unexpectedly because she hadn't heard from me, thanks to

Costin taking my phone. She's invited herself to at least a few days. Don't worry, I've told her she can't stay long, though."

"She can't stay at all."

"Why?"

Nico looked away from me and I knew he was trying to compose himself. "Why can't you be easy?" I stared back at him. "I mean," he explained, "I can't be around her."

"Then we need another plan because she wants to meet the man in my life."

"You told her about me?"

"I told her there was a man named Nico but I didn't tell her about *you*," I whispered, knowing he could hear me over the music.

Nico was silent another moment, listening to something other than the thunderous beats of rock. "She'll be back in a moment, so I need to be quick. I will see if I can borrow Costin's pet to help out. He can pose as me, so go along with any visitor that may come by your place later."

He was gone before I could ask anything about this impromptu plan. I didn't even know Costin had a pet, let alone a male one. As usual, he left me with more questions and not enough answers. Now I was going to have a stranger posing as Nico and I was supposed to what? Go along with it? My acting skills were limited. I hoped it would be enough to convince Jen.

She returned while bobbing to the music, grabbed her martini glass, and held it up in the air. "Cheers!"

I forced a smile and picked up my glass, clinking it to hers, trying to remain casual as I waited for the rest of the night to unfold. "To Florence!"

"To Italy!" She giggled.

***

Drinking and dinner ended by eleven and we were back at my apartment. Jen's stamina, she admitted, was off from the long flight.

"The jet lag should wear off by tomorrow," she swore. "Then we can do this so much better."

She began peeling clothes away before I even had the front door shut. "I'm going to bed," she announced as she unstrapped her heels.

The door to the guest room shut and I collapsed on the couch. Just as I was reaching for my book, I heard a knock on the door. I let out an exhausted sigh and pushed myself up.

I opened the front door to a handsome man in his early thirties with a schoolboy charm emanating from him. Blue eyes smiled at me as he pulled me into an embrace. "Dylan," he called into my ear. "I'm Antonio, but I'll be your

Nico for the night."

I took a step back to rid myself of the goose bumps from the warmth of his skin. "Come in," I breathed. "My friend Jen is asleep for now," I added, knowing she would probably wake sooner than later.

"You're as gorgeous as Costin said you were," he commented, sitting on the couch. My cheeks burned with a blush I knew was taking hold of my cheeks. He was pure Italian beauty with an olive complexion and short black hair that he had slicked back to show off his beautiful face. He rested his arm along the length of the back of the couch. "Come sit next to me."

He patted the couch and exposed two dimples in his tanned cheeks.

I hesitated, unsure of myself. Why couldn't any of the guys in my new life be unattractive? Nico wasn't making this easy, considering I had to pretend Antonio was him in front of Jen, which meant I had to play along now in case she came out of her room. *I can do this.*

He rested his arm on my shoulder when I joined him on the couch and pulled me a little closer to him. "I'm going to keep whispering, so we can get to know each other and make it look as natural as possible in case your friend decides to join us, yes?"

"Okay," I whispered back, smiling at his effort to talk

softly. "So how did you get involved with Costin?"

"First, it's not what you think. We are not lovers, though many others in town will tell you differently." He sounded very defensive about this. I wondered how many of the others teased him about this.

"I didn't mean to imply…."

He placed two fingers to my lips to quiet me. This was going to be harder than I thought. I would have to thank Nico later, I thought sarcastically. His warm skin was the biggest attraction here. It had been a while since I've been this close to another human.

"It's okay, I'm not offended. It was a natural thought."

"Can you read my thoughts?" I asked. He seemed to know everything in my head. I had thought about him and Costin as lovers before I asked the question and he knew where I was headed before I could go into detail.

"No, but your face is very expressive. I knew what you were thinking, and I was right, yes?"

I nodded.

"Costin actually found me about three years ago. I am a doctor, or was, and he found the research I was doing interesting. He watched me for about five years before he approached me."

"What did you do when you found out what he was?"

I asked, glad to find someone I could finally talk about these things with.

"I thought I lost my mind," he laughed softly. "Even so, the evidence was there and my research started to make a little more sense." Antonio stopped for a moment when he read my confusion. "You see, my research is on the dead and what makes the body actually die. I was trying to find a way a human could become immortal. When Costin offered eternity to me, I was hooked."

"When is he going to turn you?"

"I have asked to wait a little while longer. There are certain things I can research better while being human. He has left it up to me to decide when. I figure within the next few years, I'll be ready. And you?"

I looked up at him. "Nico has said within the next year. We have run into some problems with others in the area trying to…err…stake claim. How long have you been his pet?"

"Almost three years. Costin says you haven't been marked yet. What's holding you up?"

"Well," I sighed. "It's been crazy lately. Nico's never marked anyone before, so he's a little hesitant. I can't say I'm excited about it, either."

Antonio smiled. "It's nothing to worry about. It hurts at first, but once the initial pain is through, it's actually pleasurable." I could tell he was a little embarrassed to admit this, since he was talking about Costin.

"Really?"

He nodded. "Something about the bite, it's very sensual. It can be better than sex." It was his turn to blush. I laughed a little, though I didn't think he was being completely serious with me. "I've let Costin bite since then. It is a feeling I don't think I'll ever grow old of."

I pulled back a little to look at him. His bronzed skin was taut across his face and he grinned at me. "I can't imagine."

"Let me show you," he said, moving my hair away from my neck. His fingers traced the lines of my neck and his warm breath came closer to my skin. "Usually right here," he whispered, pressing his lips to the base of my neck, "or here." He moved his mouth just below my earlobe.

I pushed myself off the couch, removing myself from the temptation. He just met me, and while yes, he was supposed to be Nico, he *wasn't* Nico. I went to the kitchen and poured myself a glass of Chianti.

Antonio came up behind me. "I upset you."

"Not upset me, but...." I let the thought go unfinished. I didn't know how to tell him to back off without offending him.

"I came on too strong?" He backed up from me a

little and poured himself a glass of wine.

I nodded. "It's fine if Jen is here because she'd expect it, but otherwise...."

"It's just, well, Costin shares me, so I figured Nico shares you."

I tried to hide my shock in his words. "What do you mean Costin shares you?"

"He lets me have my own life. I can see women and sometimes if there is a visiting sovereign, I will supply them." Antonio said all this nonchalantly and I had to think about what he was saying.

"Supply them? As in, let them bite you?" I whispered. I was surprised Antonio was okay with all this. I hadn't thought of it until now. Now I had more questions.

He made a small hand gesture to dismiss my naivety. "In this community, touching isn't as intimate as humans make it out to be. It's really not a big a deal. It is a small sacrifice for eternity, don't you think?"

"My relationship with Nico is a little different. I don't think he plans on sharing me."

"Oh." I watched his face absorb what I was trying to say. "So the two of you," he trailed off. "Ohhh." He finally realized what I was telling him.

I turned to hide the embarrassment I knew was written all over my face. Why had he expected Nico and I weren't intimately involved? Is this the first time it's been done? I found it hard to believe but I wasn't going to talk to Antonio about my sex life, so I tried for some silence for a while.

I heard a sound from down the hall and before I could react, Antonio wrapped his arms around my waist. As I craned my head around the corner to see Jen trotting towards us, he buried his head in the crook of my neck.

"I thought I heard voices," she announced as she came into view and letting out a yawn. She raised her eyebrows as she watched Antonio nuzzle at my neck.

"Hey Jen," I said, pulling out of Antonio's grip a little. "I'd like you to meet…Nico."

Antonio released me and took a step towards Jen. "Great to meet you," he held out his hand in greeting.

Jen smiled and glanced over at me, giving me her 'I approve' look. "Nice to meet you."

We walked into the living room and she curled up in the seat across from where we sat on the couch. Antonio still kept a firm arm around my shoulder and his other hand on my knee. Jen couldn't get the grin off her face. We talked for about an hour before Antonio finally excused himself for the night.

"Bring a friend tomorrow," Jen giggled as I closed the door.

"So?" I asked as I walked back into the living room. I was making sure she had accepted the hoax we dealt in front of her.

"Nice. I see you've moved on as well, and I'm glad."

"I have," I smiled, "Way on. Now, I'm turning in for the night."

Chapter 16

"IS SHE GONE?" Nico asked when he cautiously entered my apartment.

"For now, yes. She's out with a friend of Antonio's. He stopped by earlier to pick her up and introduce her. He figured it would give us some alone time." I shut the door behind us. "I'm supposed to meet them down at a club later."

"Remind me to thank him," Nico commented. He took a step closer to me to close the distance between our lips.

The apartment was quiet except for the traffic sounds outside. I needed a fountain or something that would make some more noise. I couldn't handle being the only thing who made sound in this place.

"Your friend believes that you and Antonio are a

couple?"

"Yes, Jen thinks that he is way out of my league, but he does a good job of acting, so she bought the whole thing." I did not want him to ask for details. He had to know Antonio would have to get close to me for Jen to believe we were dating on such a level that I moved into his apartment.

"Good. Did Antonio go too far?" He asked. I knew he'd have to ask for at least some details. I was getting used to his jealous side and it made me feel more secure in our relationship. It was endearing, though I wondered why he felt the need. Any sane girl would only have to take one look at him and be hooked.

My stomach was cramping and I realized it'd been a while since my last meal. I made my way to the kitchen cabinets with Nico close on my heels and waiting for my answer.

I pulled down the crackers and in between bites, I explained. "There was a lot of talking at first. Jen was asleep when he first arrived. When she showed up, I think we were convincing."

"And what kind of convincing did it take?" He asked, his voice raising an octave.

I considered dragging out the details a little to find out the degree of jealousy that Nico had, but thought better of it. "There was touching, but we never kissed."

"Touching?" He asked, watching my every move. It would be interesting to see how things would play out if Nico ever thought Antonio took things too far. The rule was you could not harm another vampire's pet...however there were always exceptions. Would he have to get Costin's permission? Antonio was harmless, as far as I could see, so hopefully it would never come to blows.

I laughed. "Yes, touching. Innocent touching," I traced my fingers along his neck as Antonio had done to me.

Nico accepted this with a small bow of his head. "All right."

"Can you explain some things to me?"

"Sure, *mia mortale*, what's the matter?"

I sat on the couch and fidgeted a little, wondering when he was going to tire of all my questions. "Why can't you be around Jen? I mean, she's my one mortal friend. She came all the way from Florida to check on me and I just thought you'd want to meet her."

He let out a sigh. "Dylan, it's not that I don't *want* to meet your friend. It's, well, I figured you would get it."

"Get what?"

"Remember the conversation we had with Henri?"

I tried remembering which one he meant and just when I was about to ask, it dawned on me. "She's B positive?"

"Yes, and I fear I might make a bad first impression if I attack her," he smiled. "It's one thing to be able to take a sip when I encounter a tourist, but it's another to be surrounded by the smell."

"Got it. Why didn't you just say so in the beginning?"

He stared at me. "I didn't want you to think I'm some sort of monster."

"I know what you are, it just goes with the territory…right?" I kissed his lips lightly.

He shook his head. "It never surprises me how accepting you are."

I laughed. "Because I'm going to change my mind about you now? After all this? Give me some credit!"

"I know I should know better. So when is she leaving?" He glanced around as though he expected her to barge through the door at any moment. Her scent was all around the apartment and I knew it was driving him crazy. He couldn't seem to sit still.

"I don't know. In a day or two, I think. Will you be able to mark me tonight?" I blurted the last part out by accident and wished that I eased into the topic a little better. I had nightmares last night of Olivier and I woke up screaming. That one was a little difficult to explain to Jen, but she finally accepted I had had too much to drink and it's what caused my fit.

"Why the sudden interest in the mark again?"

I smiled and recalled what Antonio said about the bite. "Antonio said it wasn't bad."

"Really? What did he say about the mark?"

"He said it can be better than sex."

Nico raised his eyebrows. "I doubt that, but it's an interesting theory. What else did the two of you talk about?"

"He told me about how Costin shares him. He thought you would share me, too."

"Oh?" His brow dropped a little and I couldn't quite read his emotions. "I do not like the sound of that, Dylan."

"Don't worry. I told him I doubted you had plans to share me." I watched his face turn to a smile as he wrapped his arms around me.

"You would be correct." He shifted his weight on the couch and brought me under his arm. "Did Antonio talk to you about his research?"

"A little. It's nice to be able to talk to another human. I mean, about everything that's been going on. Someone who won't think I've lost my mind, though...."

"Yes?"

I coughed nervously. "It's just that he seemed a little surprised we were intimate. It's certainly not the relationship he and Costin have."

There was a soft laugh and then silence for a moment.

"As for the intimacy, it's true – what we are doing is not common." He said it wasn't common, not unheard of. That was encouraging. I'd hate to think we were the only ones to be intimately involved.

"And the other part?" I had to ask by the way he casually omitted any comments to the last part. Was there something Antonio wasn't sharing?

Nico shifted uncomfortably and finally settled for standing. "I am not one to talk about my sovereign's love life, though what he has shared sounds a bit more intimate than what Antonio has perhaps told you."

I let it soak in for a minute. "Hmmm." I wondered if Antonio was embarrassed to tell me he was intimate with another man or if he didn't consider certain things as Costin might. I was thinking of ways I could approach the subject without alarming Antonio to my curiosity.

"Now for the sharing – I have heard Costin shares Antonio with others. Antonio allows friends of Costin to drink from him and he quite enjoys it."

"Do you want to drink from me?" I asked nervously. I knew my voice went up a pitch when I asked but I hoped he hadn't noticed.

He smiled, flashing his fangs for an instant. "Are you offering?"

"It depends…" I didn't know how to approach this

subject. Antonio and I talked about this subject a few times throughout the night and he said it was my duty as a pet to offer blood to my maker, as he put it. When I told him Nico hadn't drunk from me yet, he was shocked.

Had I been denying Nico something I should have been offering? He hadn't said anything, though maybe he was waiting for me to offer. Maybe it was something that he expected of me once I was marked.

"Depends on what?" He seemed to be deep in thought, wondering what it was I was going to say to allow him to drink from me. I could tell the excitement of this possibility was lying just below the surface of his cool exterior.

"Do you *want* to drink from me?" I asked. Maybe he didn't even want to. After all, O positive wasn't even his favorite.

He made a gesture with his hand. "Is this a trick question?" I shook my head. "That's like me asking you if you'd like a glass of wine or a piece of chocolate. You'd never refuse it."

I grinned at the way he phrased it. There it was. He wanted to drink from me and I hadn't offered…yet. I wasn't sure if I'd like it as much as Antonio told me I would. How much would he even take? Would it be a few ounces or a pint? I was trying to remember how much I used to give during blood donations.

"Dylan," he cooed. He had one arm on either side of my head, leaning his weight into the back of the couch. "Don't worry so much. I will mark you before I ask to drink from you. Okay?"

I nodded. "Okay."

He got up and paced in front of me in an attempt to get the scent of Jen out of his head. From his reactions, you'd think her blood had spurted out and dripped on everything in here.

"Do you want to go somewhere?"

He was at the front door before I could even blink. "I thought you'd never suggest it." He held the door for me. "Let's go."

"Can we go to your place?" It was one of the many things that were still a mystery to me. I hadn't seen where he slept at night, or even been told where it was.

Nico shut the door to my apartment and studied me for a few minutes. I stood there under his scrutiny while I watched a million thoughts race across his face.

"Olivier's in Paris," I added to remind him that he didn't have any valid excuses to deny me yet again.

Finally, he nodded. "Come." He scooped me into his arms.

After leaping several dozen rooftops, we walked

down a narrow road where loose stone scattered the ground and faded paintings were etched on the walls. The road ended into a large wooded area. I stood there and compared his version of flight compared to Pablo's. It wasn't quite as smooth and I wondered if it was an age thing or a skill that hadn't been acquired. Nico broke my train of thought before I had a chance to ask.

"I need you to close your eyes," he said, coming to a stop.

"Why?"

"You can't see where I live. I can take you on the inside, but I can't have you see the outside or how to get there. Not until you've been turned."

I rubbed the back of my head and knew he was going to be frustrated with my next question. "Why?"

"Because...," he sighed. "Other vampires could find me and until you're turned, they can easily pull that from your mind."

Well, that was a good reason. I had more questions, but I humored him and closed my eyes.

He gathered me into his arms and we were off again. The wind was in my hair and I clung close to him, my eyes sealed tight. I could feel the brush of branches against my arm and as I was about to ask how much longer, a heavy wood door creaked open and he set me down.

"Now?" I asked, standing with my eyes still closed, hands on my hips.

"Now."

I opened my eyes to what could have been a giant bed and breakfast. "Wow." I was speechless. This place was absolutely gorgeous and couldn't figure out why I wasn't living here instead of an apartment some twenty minutes away.

"Would you like a tour?"

I nodded, following closely behind. "How old is this place?" I asked, admiring the tall walls of solid white stone.

"It was built in the 13th century as a mill. I bought it sometime in the early 1800s once it had been converted to a house. Then, about fifty years ago, I had electric and plumbing installed."

"It's amazing, though…." I trailed off. I stared at the wooden rafters above my head and the spacious areas.

"Yes?"

"I love the apartment, but I really wish I could have stayed here."

"Why did you put me up in the apartment instead of letting me stay here?"

He laughed. "I know you would have, but it's just not safe. Besides, this place is very far out of the way."

"Will it really be safe when I'm turned, though?

Costin can read your mind."

"Yes, but it is because he is my sovereign. Reading thoughts are limited to those in your line, meaning those who make you or who you've made, as well as your sovereign."

"Really?" I asked as I started to climb the wooden staircase in the corner. "So I'll be able to read your thoughts?"

"Yes," he spoke, and I knew he was right behind me.

"Won't that be fun!" I turned on the stairs to see his reaction.

Nico flashed a smile. "I'll have to be careful is what it means."

"So, can I ask more questions? I've been trying to be good and wait for them to be answered, but—"

"Of course," he pulled me into his arms as we reached the top of the landing.

The second floor was one giant room with a large bay window overlooking the Arno. He led us to the couch that was positioned in front of the breathtaking view. From here, I could see all the twinkling lights of Florence and wondered how much different it would look during the day, though I knew I wouldn't get to see it.

Nico rested his arm around my shoulders and waited for my questions to begin.

"How can you afford my apartment? Do I need to

start paying you rent? I mean I can pick up more nights at the bar."

"Don't be ridiculous. You don't even need to work if you choose not to."

I took a deep breath, trying to keep my constantly growing list of inquiries in check. "How?"

"Okay, I have made you wait long enough for your answers. I have told you I'm almost three hundred years old, yes?"

"Yes."

"That is almost four lifetimes to earn money. I have made very good investments over the years, I own a lot of real estate throughout Italy, and interest is a wonderful thing."

"But you don't put the money in a bank, do you? I mean, they'd get suspicious if you've had a bank account open for over a hundred years, right?"

"I have a very trustworthy lawyer who manages my affairs. He doesn't know exactly what I am, but he is paid very well not to ask questions. His father helped me, and his father, and…well you get the idea."

I nodded, listening. I was glad to finally get the burning questions that have been in and out of my mind since I moved into the apartment. "So you do have a bank account?"

Nico smiled, knowing I was on a roll with questions. He was trying to be as patient with me as possible, and he was actually answering without hesitation.

"Yes. It's under a false name and every fifty years or so, the account is closed and re-opened under a new name."

"What's the name it's under now?" I was waiting for some ordinary name like John Doe.

"Nico," he said, blankly. "What else would it be under?"

I opened my mouth to say something and closed it again. I was expecting something more complicated than just his name. That was just too easy. "Really?" I finally asked, waiting to see if there was something I missed.

"Really. The last name is Marionelli right now, but it changes every so often. Sometimes it is Nico Marionelli the second or third, but yes, it is simple. It's easier to remember." He seemed amused by how surprised I was at this new knowledge.

He kissed the side of my cheek and we looked out over the night for several minutes before he turned to me again. I was looking for the Duomo or some sort of landmark, trying to figure out where we were. I knew we were east of the city, but that was it.

"Were those all the questions you had for me?"

I nodded absently. "For now. I could ask a few

hundred more, but I can wait. At least I know you can afford my apartment now."

"Yes, it is something you don't need to worry about."

I did still want to work because it was something to do and I enjoyed it. I knew, though, that Matt needed a visa from me soon so he could put me on the books. "Well, it reminds me…if I'm going to be staying, I need to apply for a visa or citizenship or something. My travel visa is only good for ninety days." I had been thinking about this on and off for about two weeks now and I knew I had to get it taken care of. I didn't even know how to start the process.

"Well, I guess now is as good a time as any."

"What are you talking about?"

"Close your eyes."

I saw Nico reaching into his back pocket and he paused when he saw that my eyes weren't shut yet. I humored him and shut them.

"Now hold out your hand."

I held out my right hand and felt a piece of paper fall into my palm. I fingered the papers. "Can I open them?"

"Yes."

I looked at the papers, all very legal looking. I looked up for some sort of interpretation to all of this. "I'm gonna need some help here."

"You're an Italian citizen now. I had my lawyers draft

it earlier today." He grinned with pride.

A citizen? I felt Nico staring at me, most likely trying to gauge my reaction. I wanted to be happy, but something wasn't quite right.

"Your papers will help for a couple different reasons. You won't be known under your current name, you're now legal to work, and we won't have to worry about you getting thrown out after your ninety-day visa expires."

"Well that all certainly helps." I peered through the documents, looking for a name.

"What are you looking for?"

"The name that I'll be known as."

Nico pointed to the top of the second page. "Your first name, my last name."

"Oh."

"Just oh?" His eyebrow raised.

I shrugged. "Honestly, I don't know what to say. I mean, how did you get all this done?"

"You worry too much. My lawyers drafted it up at my request. As far as the Italian government is concerned, you and I are married so you could become a citizen." He said this so matter-of-factly so I barely caught the last part.

"Married?" I blurted out before I could contain my reaction. "Excuse me?"

Nico put his arm around my shoulder. "Dylan, it's

just paperwork. Please don't make more out of this than it needs to be. Besides, it changes your last name so your friends or anyone else can't look you up. It was the easiest way to get the paperwork filed."

"How romantic," I commented dryly. I never thought I would get married again – not after Chris. Being involved with vampires was supposed to be easier, at least from that standpoint. I bit my bottom lip, trying to figure out how to explain all this to Nico. He was just trying to help and I would be eternally grateful, but marriage was a big step that I didn't want to take, even if it was just on paper.

Nico wrapped his arm tighter around me and kissed my temple, leading me downstairs. "Please do not be angry. I did it for us."

"So I'm Dylan Marionelli now?" I thumbed through the paperwork to see it in print.

Nico smiled. "Yes you are."

"Hmmm," I said. I'd need more convincing. Mindlessly, I looked down at my left hand and noticed the severe lack of any hardware to go with my new last name. Why did I care that there was no ring there? It was just supposed to be paperwork. If he had wanted to marry me, he would have asked me. So why did I feel the sudden urge to cry?

We reached the bottom of the stairs and he hesitated

by the front door. "It is late and I need to get you back."

I nodded, staring at the floor.

"What am I missing?"

"What do you mean?"

"I've upset you in some way?"

I looked past him instead of at him. "No, it's fine."

Nico shook his head. "I may not be around women often, but I know that fine is not a good thing."

I wiped at my eyes and stood up tall. "Truly, I'm fine."

"Did you want a ring?"

"What?"

He gestured at the papers in my hand. "We are married. Would a ring be appropriate?"

I chewed on my bottom lip before shaking my head. "No. It's just paperwork." Once I said it, I started to believe it. In time, I could get used to the idea. It was so I could be in the country legally. Italy was now my home. The sooner I accepted it, the sooner I could move on.

"We should get you back. Jen may wonder what happened to you."

Right. I secretly hoped she was planning a late night with Antonio's friend so I could have some time with Nico after the club. I wanted to enjoy his company and it wasn't going to happen if she was there. She just had to have a blood type that only like one out of every fifty Americans have. It was so like Jen to always be the unique one.

"Okay," I managed as I followed him down the staircase. I really liked the old feel of this place and thought it would make a great bed and breakfast. He had interests that kept him busy during the nights, like a job. Real estate was his thing. What would I do to pass my nights once I became a vampire? Maybe I could convince him to move and turn this place into a bed and breakfast. I have the restaurant experience.

I'd have to remember to ask him about my idea one day. I had more than enough time.

As we made our way back into the city center, we paused outside of a very loud, very bright night club. He seemed to be waiting for something.

"Why did we stop?" I looked around for some reason to be here.

"Antonio should be here any minute. You and he are going to go in and hang out with Jen and her date. That way there are no questions."

Nico was a little too good at this game of charades. He reached in and kissed me. I wrapped my arms around his neck and brought him a little closer. I did not want to stop.

"Ahem."

I looked up to see Antonio standing beside us and

waiting to usher us inside.

"Hi," I said as I moved away from Nico.

Nico traced a finger down my cheek. "I'll see you tomorrow." I watched him walk around the corner of the building until he was gone.

"Shall we?" Antonio asked, holding his elbow out to me.

I took his arm and walked in.

***

"No wonder you don't want to leave Italy!" Jen whispered when she yanked me towards the bathroom with her. The women pressed in among us were applying lipstick in the mirrors and spraying perfumes on each other. We were given a few sideways glances as the two of us stood along the far wall.

"The date is going well?" I asked. I was glad that Eduardo had made that quick of an impression.

Jen shook her head and eyed me as she readied to admit something. "No…well, yes, but that's not what I mean."

"What do you mean, then?" I wasn't sure where she was going with this conversation and I certainly wasn't going to offer up anything extra.

"Two men! I didn't think you had it in you."

A woman applying lipstick in the mirror pushed her wavy brown hair behind her ear and turned from the mirror to look at me.

"Wh-what?" I stuttered, trying not to hyperventilate in the crowded bathroom. Women shoved past us to the lines in front of the stalls. I didn't know she had seen Nico, the real Nico, and I outside of the club. I thought we had been far enough from the door.

"I saw you kissing the guy outside the club," Jen gushed. "I just can't believe Nico is cool with you seeing another guy. That is just friggin' awesome!" She hesitated on something and then her eyes widened. "Are you sleeping with both of them? Together?"

I could tell I had just appealed to her biggest fantasy. I didn't see too many ways out of this one. How was I supposed to explain my kissing Nico right in front of Antonio? The only way I *could* was by going along with the scenario she had cooked up in her head. It sounded a little slutty to me, yet Jen thought it was a dream come true.

I concentrating on the red and white tiles we were standing on as I nodded to confirm her suspicions. I certainly couldn't clear things up with the truth, so I let her have her fantasies. She thought she'd live vicariously through me and my new life. I would only have to lie for a few more days until she was on the plane back home on Friday. After that, the lies wouldn't mean anything anymore, except that she would be safe from the craziness I'd involved myself in.

She grabbed me prior to jumping up and down as she shrieked in excitement. It caused a few heads to turn but she just kept hugging. Jen was the only person I knew that could get excited like this, especially over the idea of her best friend having a threesome. I never said she was the sanest person.

"I am so proud of you," she giggled as we finally left the bathroom. Antonio and Eduardo were standing outside and waiting for us. Eduardo grabbed Jen's hand almost immediately and whisked her out on to the dance floor.

Antonio led me slowly to the other side of the room so we could dance or talk. He would let me decide. I stepped in close to whisper into his ear and be heard over the loud booming of techno music. His cologne was spicy, like cinnamon, and it filled my senses. It made me take another step in before I could decide against it.

"She thinks we're sleeping together," I whispered, trying not to sound too prudish.

"Isn't that the idea?" He slid in next to me and smirked at the implications.

I shook my head. "No. She thinks you, me, *and* Nico are sleeping together."

"What?" His eyes grew a little large at this.

I nodded. "She saw us outside. She jumped to her own conclusions and rather than try explaining, I agreed."

"Nice," he said, pulling me against him as we saw Eduardo and Jen gliding across the dance floor. She had her hips pressed into his pelvis, gyrating with the music. She was so focused on her date that I don't think I even registered on her radar.

"Nice?" This was hardly what I considered nice. My best friend now believed I was sleeping with two men, which was something I could never actually do. The worst part was she believed it.

"Well, it wouldn't be the worst thing ever," he said, catching my eye.

"Oh." Before I could form a question to his comment, his lips were on mine. He stepped in close so his body was against mine and I had no doubt about his intentions, since it was pressed into my hip. "Antonio," I pulled my mouth away from his. "This is not going to happen."

"Dylan, you take yourself too seriously," Antonio announced. He pulled back enough so I could look into his face, but his arms stayed wrapped around my waist. "Ease up."

I took a step back to leave his grasp. "No, you need to back off."

"Dylan, come on!" He tried closing the distance between us again but I stopped him with a hand on his chest.

He looked at me as if I had just caused him physical pain. I stopped and stared at him, waiting for some sort of explanation.

"I'm just trying to put on a good show for your friend," he said. I heard the words coming out of his mouth but I really didn't believe it. Even as he looked at me, I knew he didn't believe them either.

"Really?" I asked. "Just a show?"

"You'd really prefer him over me? I mean, seriously? His heart doesn't even beat for God's sake!" He spat the words vehemently and moved his face as close to mine as possible.

I wasn't sure what his plan was and I didn't want to find out. He didn't understand the boundaries very well and I didn't want to try and explain them. I was about to try when I sensed someone behind me. I tensed when I spun around to find it was Nico.

"Antonio, leave." Nico advanced on Antonio as he spoke. I watched in muted fascination as the two men faced off on the edge of the dance floor.

Antonio nodded and turned on his heel. He walked as fast to the exit as he could possibly go without going into a full sprint.

"Thank you." I clung to Nico's side as several nearby women who had been watching the scene eyed him curiously. Nico grabbed me and we stepped away from the crowd.

"Are you okay?" he asked.

I nodded. "It's just that he doesn't get you and I are different than what normally goes on." I wasn't sure why I was trying to defend Antonio, but in some strange way, I understood. Costin was always sharing and being a pet was just a step towards eternity. For me, it was much more than that.

"I know. I'm going to have to speak with him, though. If he tries something like that again, Costin's going to need to step in. What started it all, anyway?"

I sighed, remembering all too clearly. As I began to explain, Nico laughed.

Chapter 17

"SO ARE WE going to talk about it?" Jen asked while sitting on the couch.

I avoided the topic as long as I could, pouring cereal into a bowl and taking a long time to get the milk out of the fridge. How she woke with this much energy was beyond me. The wine had given me a bit of a headache.

"Well?"

I looked up at her. I knew exactly what she wanted to talk about and I had absolutely no idea what to say. Nico and I didn't discuss how this was going to be handled and now I sat here on my own trying to figure it out.

I made myself comfortable on the couch knowing that she had been thinking about this all night. She smiled, eager to hear some outrageous story about the two men in my life, though she had no idea what my life was really like and that there was only one man in my life. Only one who mattered anyway.

"Talk about what?" I finally asked with feigned innocence.

She rolled her eyes at me and let out a sigh. "Which one do you like better and what's the other guy's name? He seems very protective of you."

Oh, so she noticed that. Now for a name. This was getting way too complicated and I was just hoping I could keep it all straight in my head until she got on a plane in two days. "That was Antonio." There, I'd just swap names...should be easy.

"He's hot. I mean, Nico's good looking and all, but Antonio's like steamy hot."

I smiled. She was absolutely right. "Yeah, he is. He is amazing."

"That answers it, then. He's the one you like more."

"How do you know that?"

Jen smiled. "Your whole face lit up as soon as you started talking about him. Your voice went a little hoarse and it was all I needed. He's the one keeping you in Italy, not Nico, huh?"

Okay, so maybe she was able to read me better than I anticipated. That was the part I hated about Jen. She knew me all too well. This wasn't the way it was supposed to go. She was only supposed to meet Antonio and that was it. Now the lies were getting complicated and I wished she was getting on a plane tomorrow.

"Can I meet him? I mean, I only got to see him from across the dance floor. I want to really meet him and talk to him and find out why you're so smitten because it can't be based on looks alone."

He was handsome, wasn't he? It was good to know it wasn't a vampire thing or that I was the only one who saw it.

Her meeting him, though, was going to be a problem. I couldn't have her meet him, especially because of her blood type. I wasn't sure how much control Nico really had or what to say so she could be okay with not meeting him. I thought of denying my feelings and saying it was all about Nico, who she presumed was really Antonio. I also figured that it would be hard to get the real Antonio back here with what happened earlier today without something seeming strange. I doubted that he'd want to come anywhere near me after the humiliation he suffered. I'd have to figure out a way to explain things to him somehow.

I needed a human friend in the midst of everything that's been going on and he was the only one I had who could know the whole truth. I was going to have to plead with him for forgiveness.

In the meantime, Jen wanted answers and I had to lie. "I really haven't decided who I like better. Nico is a better conversationalist."

She looked at me as if she was deciding whether or not to believe me. She shrugged. "If I had both of these guys in my life, I don't think I'd want to leave either."

"Tell me about it."

"Seriously, though," Jen said. "You're not coming back, are you?"

I shook my head. "No."

Jen didn't say anything. I didn't know if it was because she was at a loss for words or if she had seen it coming for a while. Either way, we sat in silence until there was a knock at the door.

She and I stared blankly at each other. "Are you expecting anyone?" she asked.

"No."

"Oooh, maybe it's Eduardo to come back and finish what we started on the dance floor!" She wiggled her eyebrows at me and rushed to the door.

She opened the door and came back to sit in the chair, leaving the man at the door to fend for himself. I looked over to see Antonio walking through the door. He put up a hand in an awkward greeting.

"Hi," I said, trying to sound friendly.

"Hey, can we go for a walk?"

I got off the couch. "Sure."

"Have fun, kids!" Jen giggled as we headed to the door.

***

"It's fine, really," Antonio said to me as he and I climbed the wrought iron steps to my apartment. "I overstepped and it was my fault."

I held on to his right arm as we stopped in front of the door. "Really? I mean, I guess I should have been clearer, too. I just want us to be friends. I need you. You're...." I trailed off as I searched for the right words.

"Human?" He joked.

I smiled. "Not exactly what I was going for, but yeah, that'll work, too."

We went for full theatrics as we entered the door while laughing and holding on to each other, only to the audience of an empty apartment.

"Jen?"

I called. Nothing. I glanced at Antonio, only for him to shrug.

"Did she leave a note?" he asked while stepping towards the kitchen.

I thought of Olivier and all the drama from the past few days. "You don't think that…that…!" The idea caught in the back of my throat.

Antonio interrupted me. "No. Here's a note," he waved a napkin from yesterday's pizza run. The blue ink was hardly legible around the grease stains, but he was able to make most of it out. "She's with Eduardo. He must have called her for a lunch date. She says she'll be back in an hour."

"Hmmm," I said with a grin. "An hour, my ass…"

Antonio moved onto the couch. "Well, it gives us some time to talk, if you'd like."

I nodded and took a seat in the chair across from him. "Only if I can ask some questions and get some honest answers."

He smiled. "Sure."

"Costin." The one word was enough to elicit a sigh and groan from him.

I ignored his reaction. "Are you physically involved or is it just a blood thing?" I wanted to put the myth about the two of them to rest and finally erase any mental pictures I may have developed of the two of them from my mind.

"It's, as you put it, a blood thing, though you must understand when Costin takes blood, it is erotic. He bites and I cannot help myself. I lose all inhibitions. That was my comment about it being better than sex." My face must have shown something of shock because he felt the need to explain further. "There is no sex in the traditional sense, but he and I...." He stopped to reorganize his thoughts.

"Cuddle?" I asked, amusement in my voice.

"Amusing," he retaliated. "But you could think of it like that."

I could tell the topic was embarrassing him, so I moved on to something of stronger interest. "Has Costin ever offered Nico a taste of you?"

He laughed. "I was wondering when you were going to ask this. He has offered but Nico always declines. He does not usually like to feed from people he knows."

"Oh."

I could hear Jen approaching the door from her loud voice saying her farewell to Eduardo. A grin tugged at Antonio's mouth as I threw myself at him and landed in his lap. She opened the door and my mouth was by his ear. While she thought I was whispering sweet nothings to him, I was telling him to shut up and stop laughing.

She stood in front of us, wearing a short frock dress, looking content and tired. "Hi," she announced herself.

I peeled myself away from Antonio and turned to face her. "How was lunch?"

"It went as well as the lunch I interrupted here."

Antonio wiped at his mouth and adjusted the collar of his shirt. "I can't imagine what you're referring to."

"Mmm hmmm," Jen laughed.

"I thought you would be out with Eduardo longer. You two couldn't have possibly...," I trailed off.

"Dylan!" Jen yelled. She pointed to Antonio, shot me a knowing look and then walked to her room.

"I didn't want the details."

"You weren't going to get them," she said, shutting the door.

Antonio raised his brows. "What was that about?"

I shrugged. "With Jen? Who knows."

"I'll leave you to solve the girl drama alone. I have to get back to Costin's place before he wakes."

"For more cuddling?" I laughed.

"Don't make me regret answering your questions," Antonio said. With that, he flashed a smile and walked out the door.

Chapter 18

"WHERE ARE YOU going?"

I turned around to see Jen standing in the doorway to my bedroom. I had just slipped into my ankle length boots and was running late. "I work tonight, remember?"

"Right. I'm gonna come by with Eduardo later," she said as she walked in and helped me get into my dress. She reached behind me and zipped the back of my black dress.

"Cute outfit," she commented. "I see why you wanted to get a job."

I smiled. "Tell me about it. The clothes here are amazing, but they all come with a fairly hefty price tag." I walked into the bathroom to touch up my makeup. "So, tell me more about Eduardo."

Jen leaned against the vanity and I watched her face

light up as I curled my eyelashes with charcoal mascara. "It's kinda like a summer romance. We both know it's not going to go any further than tomorrow, but it's a hell of a lot of fun."

I looked up to face her. "Have you two...?"

She shook her head. "No, but I'm hoping for it tonight. I figured it'd be the best souvenir for my trip I could ask for. It'd make for some great stories back home, too." She wagged her eye brows flirtatiously.

I just laughed. Being carefree, no matter what, was like Jen. "Alright, so Eduardo knows where the bar is?" I asked.

She nodded. "Yeah. By the way, can I raid your closet?" I could tell by the excitement in her voice that she'd been eyeing it since she got into town.

"Of course, but I don't know what will fit. You're at least a size smaller than me." She looked at me and then over at herself. She squeezed at her gut a little and stood sideways in the mirror.

"You've slimmed down a little and I've put on some, so I think we're closer than ever."

It would figure. Finally, someone to share clothes with and she's a continent away. "Help yourself. Hands off the knee high boots, though. I haven't gotten to wear them yet myself."

A low whine escaped her lips in protest but she didn't

say anything further.

***

The majority of the staff sat in the kitchen and leaned against the counter. I looked at my watch and scooped out some risotto onto a small plate, even though I saw the chef giving me a dirty look. It was the slowest night I'd seen at Yankee Bar since I started. It was already seven. A Sunday back home would have been a guarantee it was going to be slow because of people having to work on Monday, but here it was different. That said, if the place didn't fill up within the next hour, it wasn't going to. I grabbed a fork from underneath the line and shoveled the last of the risotto into my mouth before going back over to the bar.

Giancarlo was taking care of the few guys who were there. They were low maintenance frat boys who drank bottled beer and paid cash. They were having their own conversation in coded guy language, so I grabbed a cloth and started wiping down the other side of the bar.

A few more people walked into the bar carrying umbrellas. I glanced outside to see it had just started raining. A couple obviously tourists, sat down at one of the high tops closest to the bar, setting their camera equipment and backpack on the spare stool. They pulled down the bar menu and started talking back and forth about the specials. I eavesdropped a little and overheard them arguing about who was going to place the order. They must not have realized they were in an American style, bar.

I walked up to the table.

They looked up at me and the dirty-blonde husband grabbed his dictionary. I placed my hand on the dictionary. "I speak English."

"Oh, good," his frumpy wife remarked. "Can I get a Cosmo?"

I nodded. "Sure. And you?"

"Do you have Captain Morgan?" He wiped his glasses with the corner of his t-shirt.

"Yes. Do you want it with Coke?"

"Yes, thank you."

A bombshell of a woman had taken a seat at the far end of the bar. Her long brown hair rolled in waves across her narrow shoulders and her eyes were painted a dazzling shade of purple. Giancarlo tried hard to keep himself in check as he watched her in fascination as he continued conversing with the frat boys.

The bombshell caught my eye and she stared at me for half a second. I blinked and heard something in my head. I left the table of the tourists and walked behind the bar. I made the two drinks and poured a glass of Sangiovese.

"Can you bring this to her?" I asked as I handed the glass of wine to Giancarlo and nodding to Bombshell.

That seemed to break him out of his trance. "What? Oh. How do you know it's what she wants?"

I looked at him, trying to figure out what he was talking about. "She asked for it."

"When? I never saw you talk to her. And trust me, I've been watching her."

What was *he* talking about? Of course she asked for it. Didn't she? I shook my head, knowing Giancarlo must be wrong, and brought the other two drinks over to the couple.

I wanted you to bring the glass to me, Dylan.

I stopped in the middle of the bar, almost dropping my tray. How was it I heard a voice inside my head that wasn't my own? I glanced around but had already known who was talking. I didn't want to look over because there was only one kind of person that could have a power like this. I really didn't want to meet another vampire right now. As I peeked over at Bombshell, though, I knew she wasn't giving me a choice.

I walked over and stood in front of her.

Violante.

I let my mind open up a little. *How are you able to get into my head?*

She spoke out loud this time. "It's one of my

specialties. Convenient, isn't it?"

I could think of some other words for it, too, though I kept my mind shut so she couldn't extract them from my head. I wanted to ask her what she was doing here or what she wanted, yet didn't want to come off as rude. "Can I help you with something?"

She laughed softly. "No. I just wanted to see the mortal that Niccolò has chosen over me."

The jealous tone and her narrowed gaze on me were more than a little obvious. She seemed to be sizing me up. She stared at me with a fascination that was unnerving. She sat with not a hair out of place and her chocolate brown eyes watched every move that I made.

"Don't worry. Costin has already told me that you are off limits." She sipped the wine a little and looked over at Giancarlo, who was making drinks at the other end of the bar. I saw him look over and raise an eyebrow at me. I smiled at him and he quickly turned his attention back to the customers.

I watched Violante with my own quiet fascination. A female vampire. She was certainly a beauty and she knew it as she used her sex appeal to every advantage she could. I wanted to ask her some questions of her previous relationship with Nico though I wouldn't give her the satisfaction. She didn't seem to be one of my best advocates, so keeping her at a distance was probably best. I waited for her to say something or ask something that warranted her coming to see me in person. Unless it was simply curiosity as she said. I turned to greet a guest a few stools down and as I reached over to get a glass, she was gone.

You're not good enough for him. I heard her final words reverberate in my head.

I opened my mind up with the only word that summed it all up. *Bitch.* Here's hoping she heard that loud and clear.

Jen, Eduardo, and Antonio walked in and gave me a big wave. Jen had draped herself across Eduardo and made her intentions for the night obvious to anyone who was looking. Antonio smiled and sat down at the stool in front of me.

Jen ordered a round of drinks for her and Eduardo and practically sat on his lap. He had a childish grin across his face and enjoyed every moment of her. He kissed her neck as she giggled, letting her hands wrap around his neck. I let out an awkward cough and looked at Antonio.

"They've been like this all night," he commented across the bar. "I've suggested to Eduardo that they go back to his place. Soon."

"It sounds like a pretty good idea. Hey, what do you know about a Violante?"

Antonio's eyes widened. "Don't tell me that she was here."

That didn't sound good. I nodded and he cursed under his breath.

He thought for a moment before responding. "She's obsessed with Nico, or was…or something along that line. She was upset to say the least when you came into the picture, especially when Costin sent everyone the message they were to not only keep their hands off, but to protect you in the event of someone else trying to stake claim."

I wrinkled my nose a little. "So what you're trying to say is, her and I won't become best friends anytime soon?" I laughed uneasily.

"You would be correct." We both looked over at the frisky couple next to him and Antonio gave Eduardo a jab to the ribcage. "Take her to Dylan's place or to your apartment or hell, even to my house, but not here."

I laughed at his honesty to the situation. Public displays of affection always made me feel a little uneasy. I always felt like I should look away, but that's never what my eyes wanted to do.

The two of them nodded and quickly left the bar, arm in arm. Antonio reached across the bar and planted a kiss on my cheek. "I'll catch up to you later, too. Oh, and don't forget to tell Nico about Violante."

"Why?"

"Just do it."

I nodded and he left. As if I could forget about an important detail like that!

Giancarlo walked over to me with inquisitive eyes staring me down. "So, the beautiful woman at the end of the bar...."

He waited for me to offer up some information that could help him with Violante.

"I'd keep my distance from her. I get the feeling she's bad news," I said and walked out from behind the bar.

Chapter 19

IT WAS EARLY morning when I heard my bedroom door creak open. "Dylan?" Jen asked, peering into my bedroom. I was lying on the bed and staring at the ceiling just thinking, daydreaming, and absorbing everything in.

"Yes?" I asked, not bothering to sit up.

She sat down on the edge of the bed and put her hand across the comforter, right over my leg. "I'm leaving tomorrow, but I wanted to talk to you about some things first."

"Okay."

"Well, I just don't want you to think I'm intervening in your life, but...." She nervously tore at her perfectly manicured red fingernails with her teeth.

"Jen, just say what's on your mind," I commented,

trying not to sound agitated. I did feel like she'd been butting in, though I stayed silent about all that. As much as I loved having her here, she didn't belong. Olivier could show up again at any moment and she simply wasn't safe amongst the vampires. She remained in the dark about all that, but it would only be a matter of time before she learned something that could cost her dearly. I wouldn't be able to live with her if that happened, so I had to say goodbye to her.

Her timing was poor, too. I needed to ask a million questions of Antonio, but she always seemed to be within earshot. The whole charade of Nico and Antonio around her was getting harder.

"I don't want to see you get hurt, that's all." I heard the concern in her voice, but she was worried for all the wrong reasons. Had she known even a small portion of the truth, she'd realize how true her words were.

"What is all of this about?"

She sighed and laid down beside me, like her and I had done a million times before back home. "He just seems out of your league. You know I love you, but—"

"I know. I think he's out of my league, too, but somehow it works. I can't explain it." Had she actually met the real Nico face to face, she'd know how much out of my league he truly was. I still wondered how he was attracted to me and how we were able to be together. I'm glad she hadn't gotten the chance to get to know the real Nico or this conversation would be even harder.

"Do you love him?" She turned her head to look at me.

Love. That was a big word. I couldn't even begin to answer her because there was so much depth in that question. Technically, we were married, but love was not something that he and I had talked about. I suppose I did love him, even if I had no idea where he stood on the topic. Slowly, I nodded in response to her question.

"Then…never mind." Jen was trying to change the subject and avoiding eye contact with me.

I let out a tired sigh. "What?"

She hesitated, rolling her head back and forth on the pillow, not wanting to say what was on her mind. She took in a deep breath and blurted it out. "Why not ask him to come back to Florida with you?"

There it was. I had been waiting four days for her to come to this conclusion and ask. Of course she'd ask. It was a selfish thing, really. I would never ask a guy to move across the world for me, even if I had wanted it. The problem this time is that I didn't want it. I wanted to stay here. Not to mention that because of everything else going on, Florida was not even a comprehensible option. "I like it here. I feel more like myself than I ever have."

"I thought you'd say that. I can see it in your eyes. You're different. Good different, but you're not the same Dylan you were in Florida."

She had no idea how true the statement was, but I nodded in agreement. "Thank you for not pushing."

"Wouldn't you invite your friends to the wedding?" She asked. She seemed personally offended that I wouldn't invite anyone to my nuptials.

I shook my head. "Probably not. Only because I don't think I'd get married. The idea of planning another wedding makes my stomach turn. I've done it once already." Little did she know that technically I already was married, thanks to Nico.

"Dylan," she trailed off. I could tell she felt sad for me and did not know what to say. "I hate that my brother left you feeling so jaded. You can't say you will never get married just because of what he did to you."

"Jen, you don't need to feel bad or sad, it's just the way it is. Just know that I'm happy and you can return to Florida sharing that information. I'm at home here and I'm in love. It's all that matters anymore."

She stood up from the side of my bed and headed out the door. "Okay. I just get the feeling that I'm talking to you for the very last time…like you're never going to keep in touch with me ever again."

I wanted to tell her she was right and that as soon as I dropped her off at the airport tomorrow, she never would see or hear from me ever again. I wanted to tell her the truth about it, but I couldn't. "Don't be ridiculous," I lied.

Chapter 20

JEN AND I finished lunch at a little bistro around the corner from my apartment and got a taxi to pick us up from there. Our driver was a little old man with white hair and dark shades, struggling to get her suitcases in the trunk. Jen offered to put them in herself but he pointed to the backseat and kept saying, "in, in."

The taxi ride to the airport was silent, with the exception of traffic and the taxi driver singing rather loudly to some song on the radio. Jen looked at me several times as his voice cracked and squeaked as he mutilated the song. He pulled up close to the small terminal and Jen and I got out. She saved him the trouble this time and got her bags out of the back before he could. I paid the fare and asked him to wait a few minutes for me.

I walked around and held out my arms to her to come to me. "Jen."

"I'm going to miss you," Jen said, hugging me tight. I returned the gesture and choked back tears. I was surprised at how emotional I had become. I neither wanted her to go nor stay. I pulled back, wiping the back of my hand across my face. Keep it together, I told myself.

"I'll miss you, too." I lifted her carry-on so she could sling it across her shoulder. She and I stared at each other awkwardly for a moment, each of us knowing in our own way this would be the last time we'd ever see each other.

The airport was surprisingly busy this early in the afternoon. A small coffee shop just outside the terminal was swarming with people getting their java fix. We stood in front, people passing us with their bags of luggage. A small plane was taking off in the background and I glanced up at it.

Jen looked at her boarding pass and then back at me. "You and Antonio or Nico…you'll be fine whichever you choose. And don't worry, I'll let your friends know you're good. Though," she hesitated. "I'm still trying to figure out exactly what I'm going to tell them. They all knew I came here to see what happened to you. I mean, I think everyone expected you to be on the plane back home with me."

I nodded, knowing she'd smooth things over for me somehow. "Well, you've got about ten hours to figure out how you're going to do it."

"Thanks for the help," she said sarcastically, giving me a poke in the ribcage with her elbow.

She'd figure a way to tell everyone. I was confident of that. I wished that they could hear the news directly from me, but since it was impossible, she was the next best thing. "Just promise me one thing?"

"Sure," I agreed, wondering what she was going to ask and hoped that that I'd be able to comply.

"If you do get married, even if it's a year from now, let me be the maid of honor," she smiled. I had forgotten that I denied her of the role with the last debacle.

My eyes rolled at her and she smiled at me anyways. "Yeah, okay."

She peeked at her watch. "I've got to go...." She paused, not knowing what else to say.

There was nothing else *to* say. I watched her go through airport security and held up a single hand to wave goodbye as she turned around one last time. I knew I'd never see her again and that she was the last of my old life. She would go back to Florida and tell my friends that I was happy in Italy. She'd also speak of the new man I'd met and about my apartment and everything else she'd seen. They would accept it as the truth because it's all that Jen had seen. She'd bought the lies Nico and I told her, which—I justified to myself—had spared her life.

I imagined my friends grilling Jen for the details on my new boyfriend. They'd hate that I wasn't trying to bring him back to the States.

At least I knew I wouldn't have to worry about any of them anymore. They wouldn't come to find me. I could keep them safe.

***

Once home, I flopped myself across the bed and cried. I hadn't even been turned into a vampire and yet I was forced to say goodbye to my old life. I loved the fact that Jen came to find me and visit with me, but almost wished she hadn't because it made it that much harder.

I heard the front door creak open and Nico yelled his arrival.

The bed gave a little as he sat down. My head was still buried in the pillows. "I dropped her off earlier this afternoon."

He let out a sigh. "I'm sorry. I know it was hard for you to see her, but aren't you glad she came in a way? I know you were worried about how to sever ties with your friends."

"Yes." I sniffled and looked away. I didn't want him to see me get emotional about this. He felt bad enough about everything else that was going on, I didn't want to add to his stress as well.

"I do have some fun planned for us tonight," Nico said, pulling me into his lap.

I raised my eyebrows. "Oh?"

Nico nodded. "After all the chaos that's been going on, I thought you could use a way to relax. There's a wine tasting going on around the Piazza Santa Maria Novella. We could take a walk over there after dinner. This way you can finally learn about some more of the wonderful wines we have in Italy."

"Something fruitier?"

"I told you Italian wine isn't fruity. It's aged in oak barrels, so there will never be a sweet, fruity taste to the wine."

"In Florida," I said. "We have citrus wine. It's made with almost as much sugar as fruit."

"That sounds disgusting. Here, we use the Sangiovese grape. Depending on the region it comes from and what other grapes it is mixed with determines the actual name of the wine."

I climbed out of his lap and headed to the bathroom so I could reapply some makeup. Crying didn't leave me with much. "Where can we grab a bite to eat first?" I called out while applying eye liner.

"There's a trattoria down the road from the wine tasting. I heard a couple talking about the wild boar ragout on the menu and thought you might want to try it out."

I popped my head out of the bathroom to catch his eye. "Did this couple perhaps run into someone who needed a few sips for the night?"

Nico laughed and put his hands up. "I plead the fifth."

After putting a few finishing touches on my hair, I was ready to go. "Feed me and teach me about wine!" I said with a smile.

"My pleasure, mia mortale."

***

"Do you really have to go to work tomorrow?"

"I do, why?"

Nico shook his head. "I wanted your company."

My lips met his. "You have my company now."

He flipped me onto the bed and I allowed him because the wine had gone right to my head. "That I do."

"Whatever are you going to do to me?" I giggled.

He began plucking buttons open down my chest. "Wait and see my love, wait and see."

Chapter 21

I LACED UP my new leather knee high boots and paired them with a denim skirt and my black button down blouse for work. I was hoping the boots weren't going to kill me even though I knew I wasn't working until close, so that saved me a little. Luckily, Matt had too many people on the schedule tonight so I got a call earlier today asking if I would come in to open and then leave after the first rush. I was happy to.

The shelves were stocked and ready to go after I added a few bottles of Sambuca, rum, and tequila from the back. Giancarlo wasn't working until later so I got stuck opening up with Maria, who was still in training. She didn't know what she was doing and her too tight t-shirts were beginning to grate on my nerves, especially when it interfered with my tips.

An early bar patron sat at the end of the bar. He ordered beer and ate the lime garnish out of the bottle. Maria was smiling and giggling in front of him but he didn't seem to find her of interest. After a few minutes of being ignored, Maria finally came back over to start slicing fruit for the bar.

"Can you get more cherries from the back?" I asked her as I made a mental note of everything else we still needed.

She stared blankly at me. I guessed she didn't know exactly what I said and I knew my speech wasn't coming out too fast. I also didn't know how to say cherry in Italian so I settled with pointing to the glass jar and saying, "more." She nodded and scampered off to the back.

I caught Matt looking over at the bar and I shot him a playful scowl. He knew I hated working with her but I think he got some sort of kick out of watching me deal with her. *Sadist.* He flashed me his million dollar smile and turned on his heel back to the dining room before I could hurl a bottle at his head, which I held high above in threat.

I was looking forward to leaving early tonight because Nico and I were supposed to catch up on some lost time. Butterflies leapt around in my stomach at the thought because I was looking forward to being alone with him again. Privacy with him had been so limited over the past week because of Jen. It had been taking its toll on me with trying to keep Antonio and Nico separate for her to buy all the lies we fed her. A night alone together was what I needed to put it all to rest.

Maria returned with the jar of cherries and the guy at the end of the bar raised his bottle, silently asking for another one. She grabbed a new bottle from the small cooler and was trying to get the lid off. I watched in silent amusement as she struggled with it and wondered how she was ever going to survive a busy Saturday night. I walked by her and grabbed the bottle out of her hand. I popped the lid off on the side of the bar with one quick movement and handed it to the man who was choking back a laugh.

"Trainee?" He asked with a low chuckle.

"You think?" I joked back.

He smiled. "I'm sorry."

I shrugged. "Ahh, it's okay. I've dealt with worse."

"The name is Blake," he said, reaching across the bar with his hand extended.

I shook it. "Dylan. Nice to meet you."

"Dylan? Really?"

I rolled my eyes. "Girls can have the name, too."

He laughed. "Heard that too many times, huh?"

Maria was watching me so I continued talking to the man. After a short conversation, I learned Blake was an investment banker on business from London. He and I would periodically look back at the struggling trainee, who had lost interest in the two of us and was now trying to seduce a young college boy of maybe twenty. We both knew he didn't stand a chance. The poor guy wouldn't even know what hit him.

Blake and the college boy were the last of the pre-rush patrons. The crowds hit hard and fast tonight. I pushed Maria to the well to pour all the shots until the rest of the staff showed up. She threw a little hissy fit, not wanting to be where she couldn't be seen. After stomping her feet and mumbling some choice Italian under her breath, she settled into a decent pace of placing shots on the bar. After she made them, I'd either pass them out or light them on fire for as much flair as I could without a partner.

Giancarlo walked in just as the lines at the bar were getting uncomfortably long. He raised his eyebrows at Maria, who had her head down, her mouth shut and was pouring shots at a fairly normal pace.

"Just in time," I said to him, washing my hands at the little sink. "Your turn."

As I was about to head out from behind the bar, he grabbed my wrist and chuckled. "Where do you think you're going?"

I dusted my hands off in front of him. "I'm done for the night. Matt said I would open and then get out when relief showed up. You're my relief."

"You're leaving me with her?" Disgust was evident in his voice.

"Sorry," I whispered.

Maria tossed an empty tequila bottle into the garbage and glared at us. "I hear you," she commented with extremely thick English. "I know what you say."

My lips quivered as they held back a grin. "Gotta go," I touted as I made a quick break for the back door.

Within minutes of walking out the back door, I had Nico beside me.

"Hey."

I grinned. "Hey yourself."

"Are you ready for tonight?"

I took a deep breath. Tonight was going to be the mark. No matter how much we talked about it and no matter how much Antonio told me it would be erotic, it still made my knees weak. "Sure."

"Before we go to the apartment, however, I want to talk to you about something," Nico said, pulling at my arm so we went in the opposite direction.

"Um, okay." The night was already dark, but South Centro was lit up with the street lights and the lights from all the little trattorias. The smell of pizza pouring from the wood burning ovens was intoxicating.

Nico squeezed my hand. "That man." It was a statement, not a question.

"What man?" There weren't any people along the route that we took that stood out.

"The man in the bar that you shook hands with. You seemed to be flirting."

I stopped short to find Nico with a very serious face. He had never really been the jealous type before. "Blake? He was just a customer."

Nico shook his head in disdain. "You even know his name?"

"Yes, I ask the names of a lot of my customers. It gives me better tips." He didn't seem too convinced. "Really. You have nothing to worry about."

We were in front of the fountains of the Uffizi. It was late enough that most of the students had retreated from the night and the palazzo was almost to ourselves.

"Take a seat."

I let out a sight but complied anyway.

Nico turned his back to me and reached into his pocket. He fished out a box and turned around again. The box popped open and I heard myself gasp.

"Perhaps if you had this on your finger, he wouldn't have flirted back."

"Nico," I choked between sobs.

He slid the ring onto my left ring finger. "We got married before I could ask you properly. I'm hoping you love me as much as I love you, mia mortale. Will you wear the ring?"

I stared down at the blue diamond that was encrusted with what looked like hundreds of white diamonds around it. It was in a white gold setting and looked absolutely stunning. "Yes, of course. I love you, too." My lips met his and I flung my arms around his neck.

"Do you like the blue diamonds?" he whispered.

"I do, they match your eyes."

"I'm glad."

I stayed glued to his neck for a few more moments, breathing in his scent. If nothing else, it was now he and I against the world. This was what I wanted, even if I hadn't known it until now.

"Now I have something else I must tell you." He led me by the hand so we could continue down the road to get to the apartment.

"Nothing could top this," I said, holding his hand with my right hand and staring down at the ring, feeling content for the first time in a long time.

We walked in silence until Nico opened the front door.

***

"Costin has requested to watch me mark you tonight."

I stared at Nico and tried to figure out why Costin would want to sit in on this very intimate affair. Costin actually walked in after the last time I was supposed to be marked, though, so I knew exactly why. This situation couldn't get more awkward.

Nico smiled. "He wants to make sure we don't get carried away again."

"So he wants to be in the room when you mark me?" I rubbed the palms of my hands across my face, wanting to wake from this nightmare. "Does he have to?"

Nico nodded. "Apparently he has been talking with Henri and they're not sure how much longer your Parisian admirer is going to keep behaving. Costin doesn't want to see any harm come to you and me marking you is the best chance of honoring it."

"What a way to celebrate."

"I'm sorry, Dylan."

I waved my hand to dismiss his concern. "It's okay. I mean, it's not ideal, but I know why he's doing it. When will he be here?"

"He should be here any minute," Nico answered as

he moved closer to me. "I'm sorry it has to be this way."

A knock on the door let us know Costin had arrived. This was going to happen. Antonio told me it was a great feeling and better than sex. As I stared at Costin, I couldn't help but form a mental picture of him and Antonio in a lover's embrace with Costin nibbling on his neck.

"Dylan?" He broke my wandering thoughts.

I shook my head and I feared it was too late. They both saw the image I had conjured up. Cursing myself silently, I turned my attention to them.

"Antonio is right," Costin pointed out. "It can be a great thing for both parties. There's nothing to be scared of." I was glad he wasn't upset by my straying thoughts. The ease of which they could pluck images and thoughts from my head was disturbing. "Do you have any questions about how this works?"

I glanced at Nico, who had seated himself in the center of the bed. He patted the mattress for me to join him.

"No, not really," I said as I took a step towards the bed. "I'm just still a little unclear about how it's different than a bite."

"Well," Costin explained, "A bite is something a vampire does to an unsuspecting mortal. You know what you're getting and you're accepting of it. Through acceptance, it is different."

"Okay," I said, still a little unsure of how to proceed. I walked to the foot of the bed, my body shaking.

"It's okay, Dylan," Nico whispered while holding his hand out to me.

A part of me wanted to ask or even beg Costin to leave and promise him we'd behave. The other part of me knew it was silly, so I climbed onto the bed next to Nico.

He looked over at Costin, who gave him a small nod, and back to me. He stroked my hair for a moment and kissed me softly on the lips before letting his mouth trail down my throat. "Are you sure?"

I nodded and tried not to look at Costin. I knew he was watching us because I could feel as though his gaze was burning into the back of my head.

"Let me hear you, *mia mortale*," he said a little louder.

"Yes," I replied, my voice breaking. "Yes, I'm sure." I shifted slightly on the bed, closed my eyes, and leaned back so my head fell into the pillows. Nico moved so he was beside me and nestled his head in the crook of my neck.

His tongue traced the pulse in my throat, resting on my jugular. My breath was getting short in anticipation the bite without fully knowing what to expect. He moved my head to the side a little and I felt his teeth graze my skin.

"Okay," he whispered through clenched teeth against me.

Before I could object, I felt a sharp pain as his fangs sank into the side of my throat. A tingling sensation replaced the pain almost immediately and I could feel the blood flowing out of me. A chill ran through my body and my mind was overwhelmed with waves of pleasure.

"Good," I heard Costin in the background. He was saying something else, but I could only focus on Nico.

The room was spinning and there was only him. His scent flooded my senses and I felt like I was drowning in honeysuckle. My body pulsated with the sensations and I rode them as best as I knew how. I kept my hands on Nico and felt his skin getting warmer to the touch. I let my hands glide down his chest as I lay victim to his bite.

Nico stayed glued to my neck and I felt his cold fingers slide lower on my body as he continued to drink from me. I was getting light-headed and thought of trying to pull away, but I was enjoying the route his fingers were pursuing. My focus was on Nico's touch and the beat of my own heart. For a second, I thought I heard his heartbeat, as well.

"Enough," Costin said faintly in the background.

A loud moan of fulfillment sounded in the room and it took me several moments to realize that it was me who had made the sound. My head was spinning and my body was reacting to what Nico was doing with his hands when I felt him being physically pulled from me.

"Enough," Costin repeated louder while forcing Nico off of me.

Nico looked as dazed as I felt as he rolled over languidly on the bed. I stared up at Costin, embarrassed by what he had witnessed but unable to move and hide. I lay beside Nico, panting, trying to catch my breath, and wondering if I was still bleeding. I felt paralyzed. I didn't see any blood, but that didn't mean there wasn't any. My neck was throbbing in small electric pulses mirroring my uneven breathing. I tried to move, yet I felt like iron weights held me to the bed.

Costin peered down at me. "He took a little too much blood – that's why you're so weak right now."

I blinked in understanding and gazed up at him.

"You should be okay in an hour or so." He turned my head gently to the side, inspecting our activities. "You're marked, though."

I relaxed. I was finally untouchable from Olivier. I reached over and touched Nico's fingertips. He jumped a little and rolled over to face me.

"Ciao," he cooed as a grin tugged at the corner of his lips. "You're delicious."

I smiled, though I wasn't sure if this was something I should be happy about. It all went back to the conversations with Antonio and sharing blood. I hadn't made up my mind if offering up my blood—the very thing which kept me alive—was such a good idea.

"You could have drained her," Costin scolded.

Drained? My heart sped a little at hearing that, not knowing if I wanted to be left alone with Nico. What if he got thirsty again and Costin wasn't there to save me or pull Nico off of me? I could see it was a struggle for Costin to break him free of me, so there was no way I would be able to. Nico wouldn't kill me on purpose…yet accidents happen.

Nico glanced up. "I didn't, though." He licked his lips once more and looked a little guilty. He wouldn't make eye contact with me right away and that made me worry, as well.

"Just be careful." They exchanged several looks I wasn't able to completely see or interpret. "I'll leave the two of you to…rest." Costin slipped out the front door with hardly a sound.

Epilogue

I WAS MUDDLING mint leaves for a mojito when I saw the brunette figure appear at the end of the bar. *Violante.* I glanced in her direction and she locked eyes with me. I heard her words inside my head.

"Find a reason to leave."

The bar was just starting to get busy. All of the barstools were already full and the dining room was on a fifteen-minute wait. My body tensed and my head swam with reasons why I'd need to leave and how I could get out of my shift.

Giancarlo passed in front of me to get to the flavored vodkas and looked up at me. "Don't look so serious, you okay?" He gave me a playful jab in the ribcage with his elbow.

I went from one side of the bar to the other to figure

out how the hell I was supposed to get out from behind the bar. There was no way I could just ask to leave – not with it this busy. The only way out was to fake being sick. Now to work on the symptoms.

Sweat was beginning to appear on my forehead from my overactive imagination. I wiped my brow and looked up at him. It was time to turn up the theatrics. I steadied my hand on the counter in front of me. "I feel horrible."

He placed the back of his hand against my head. "You don't look so well, either." He pushed past me for a moment to deal with a few customers who had crept up to my side of the bar. Two bottles of beer and a martini later and he was back at my side, pouring me one. "I can get this tonight though you owe me one." Both of us knew that he would cash in on it.

"You sure?" I asked, glad he bought the act.

He nodded. "Get some sleep."

Before I was even out of the door, Violante was at my heels. "Go to him. There is trouble."

"I figured," I commented. She was never one to sugar coat anything. "Why are you the one bringing me the message, though?"

She rolled her eyes as she looked down at me. Even with my heeled boots, she was a good two or three inches taller than I was. Her brown hair was side swept and her long eyelashes flashed up and down a few times as she spoke. "Don't worry. Your little Nico is fine. He and Costin are at your apartment discussing a plan."

Her cryptic speech was getting me to walk faster. "A plan for what?"

"I am not allowed to say." I knew that must have bothered her more than anything. She said allowed but I had a feeling it was more along the lines of she didn't know all the details to share. I was not her favorite person to begin with and now she had to walk me to my apartment. I guess we wouldn't be planning on any shopping trips together anytime in the near future.

***

I walked up the stairs to my apartment and glanced back at Violante. "Are you coming up?"

"No," she answered quickly and disappeared.

I entered in the middle of a heated discussion between Nico and Costin, which ended abruptly as soon as they saw me.

Nico walked over and stood beside me before he placed his arm around my shoulder and escorted me to the couch. Costin nodded his head in greeting at me and paced back and forth in front of the couch.

"Is someone going to tell me what's the matter?"

Costin looked tired and in need of blood. His eyes were deep-set and his hair was pulled into a sloppy ponytail. As he reached the end of the imaginary line he was walking along, he turned around and stopped. "Henri is dead."

I let his words set in. I didn't want to jump to conclusions. Henri. Dead. This could mean anything.

"Dylan? Did you hear me?" His pacing continued as he repeated the question.

I tipped my head. "Does that mean…?" I didn't want to say it out loud partly because I wasn't sure what kind of impact it would have on me. I also never wanted to say his name out loud ever again. I hoped I never had to.

"We think Olivier killed Henri," Nico shared.

"If Henri is dead by the hand of Olivier, then that makes him sovereign, right?"

Costin and Nico both nodded.

"We're not sure if Olivier was completely responsible," Costin added.

"How did he die?"

"You don't want to ask that question," Nico warned.

He was probably right so I didn't press the issue.

"The only thing that we know is that you are safe right now because of the mark. Olivier has made no additional threats toward you and with Henri dead, he is staying in Paris – presumably to claim the title of sovereign," Costin started to explain.

"There are some issues behind Henri's death, however," Nico commented, "That make things a little unclear."

Costin moved in closer to me. "We do not know what Oliver's intentions are and if he has the right to be sovereign."

"So am I safe?" Just when things started to resume normalcy, or at least as normal as my life could possibly be these days, everything came back to Olivier. It always did.

Nico wrapped his arm around me. "You will be safe as long as I have anything to do with it." He twirled the ring on my left hand absent mindedly.

"He is stronger than anyone of us expected but we don't think he was working alone," Costin stated. The room spun with this new information. I took a seat on the couch to steady myself.

"So," I asked, "This means other vampires have helped him to kill Henri? Why would they do that?"

Nico clasped his hand over mine. "Vampires are not the only thing that goes bump in the night, *mia mortale*."

"You are safe because of the mark, so take comfort in that fact," Costin remarked.

ABOUT THE AUTHOR

Shannon Bell grew up in Florida and has always dreamed about vampires – and still secretly hopes they exist. She is married to someone who tolerates her crazy story-telling about Romania and has a daughter she hopes will have the same enthusiasm for vampires when she grows up that her mommy does.

Shannon has a Bachelor's degree in Creative Writing from the University of Central Florida and is a full-time writer. She's currently hard at work on her next novel.

Made in the USA
San Bernardino, CA
17 December 2013